To Michel

Awaken

The Patronus
Book One

Sarah M. Ross

Sarah M Ross

4 Corners Press

No Boundaries

4 Corners Press
- Arizona -

Published in the United States by 4 Corners Press.
www.4cornerspress.com
4 Corners Press design is a registered trademark of 4 Corners Press

Printed in the United States of America

Cover Formatting by Donna Dull of 4CP

Copyright © 2012 by Sarah M. Ross
ISBN-13: 978-1469922751
ISBN-10: 1469922754
LCCN: 2012931113

All rights reserved.

Without limiting the rights under copyright reserved above, no part of this publication may be reproduced, stored in or introduced into a retrieval system, or transmitted, in any form, or by any means (electronic, mechanical, photocopying, recording, or otherwise) without the prior written permission of both the copyright owner and the above publisher of this book.

This is a work of fiction. Names, characters, places, brands, media, and incidents are either the product of the author's imagination or are used fictitiously. The author acknowledges the trademarked status and trademark owners of various products referenced in this work of fiction, which have been used without permission. The publication/use of these trademarks is not authorized, associated with, or sponsored by the trademark owners.

Dedication

For my sister, who refused to let cancer steal her away.

One

The last thing I remembered was belting out Bon Jovi's "Livin' on a Prayer" while driving down I-95 with my best friend Janice. Two friends enjoying the sweet taste of freedom that summer brought with the windows down and the music up. It was my last weekend before I graduated college and had to join the real world. Finals were almost over, and the only one I had left was Advanced Calculus with Dr. Henry. I would worry about that later because right now, it was all about friends, sun, and surf. Our road trip to the beach was one last tryst of splashing in the ocean and soaking up the sun in our tiny bikinis before admitting we were truly grownups – taxes and 401K's and all.

But gradually the realization dawned that I was no longer in a car. And there wasn't any music. Instead, I only heard low whispers all around me. Slowly, I pried open my eyes and looked around; I realized, with growing anxiety, I didn't recognize anything. Or anyone.

"What happened? Where am I?" I asked the people hovering around me. "Is this a hospital or something?"

Gazing around the room, there were other people with me, a few men and a woman. They all looked too young to be doctors and certainly weren't dressed like it. The guys were dressed normally in loose fitting jeans and tee shirts. The woman standing next to me certainly wasn't a nurse or doctor either. She was wearing a sea green baby-doll dress with lace adorning the capped sleeves and a single ruffle cut on a bias going from her V-neck line to her waist. Confusion overtook my thoughts and panic began to set in. Something was wrong. Did I have an accident?

"You're okay now," a deep voice drawled next to me. I looked at the man who said this and my heart fluttered a bit. He was gorgeous. It was hard not to stare at him. Thick black hair that curled at the ends hung shaggily over his face, but it was just short enough I could still see his piercing ice-blue eyes. They were the clearest blue I'd ever seen, and against his dark hair, they stood out as the centerpiece on his chiseled face. He smiled at me and I could make out a small, but deep, dimple on his left cheek. I instantly felt safer when he smiled, but I didn't know why. He sat on the edge of the bed next to me, leaning in to check something on my face. Instinctively, I tried to raise my hand to see for myself, but I couldn't raise my arms. The panic I already felt deepened, and some of the monitors began beeping more quickly as my heart raced.

"Shh, it's okay," that deep voice said again, and it was enough to make me shiver. "I know you're confused, but we're here to help you with that. My name's Max. I'm going to press a button to release your arms now."

I looked down. My arms were encased in hollow tubes that looked like giant blood pressure cuffs. Their scratchy surface made my arms itch as I tried to move. Glancing further down, my legs had the same machine on them, and I wasn't wearing anything more than a sports bra and underwear with no sheet to cover me. Immediately my cheeks blushed and with my arms free, I covered what little I could just using my hands while I frantically looked for more clothes or something to cover up with.

Giggling quietly, the girl reached into a cabinet and pulled out a thin blanket and covered me. "Guys, why don't you give us girls a few minutes? She needs a little more space." The two guys standing next to her nodded silently and proceeded out. I looked at the man sitting on the bed with me and began to fidget when he took his hand and smoothed down a stray strand of hair next to my face.

"We'll be waiting just outside," Max said. "Cassie will help you get dressed and out of bed." He stood up and began to walk away slowly, almost reluctantly. It wasn't until he stood I realized how tall he was. Being 5 feet 11 inches, I had a tendency to size people up, even from a distance. He was definitely taller than me, and if I had to guess I would say he was at least 6 foot 5. As my eyes drifted down to his backside, the monitors begin to beep faster again. I immediately felt embarrassed and glanced away.

Cassie smiled. "Don't worry, I don't know a whole lot of people whose heart wouldn't skip a few beats while staring at Max. I've even caught myself doing it! Don't tell Adam though, he tends to get jealous." She pressed a few buttons, and the giant cuffs slid off of my legs. "Here, let me help you out of those leg pumps and get you standing up." She put her forearm under my armpit and tried to raise me up.

"Hold on, I don't understand," I pulled back, resisting her efforts. "What is going on? Who are you people? Where is my family?"

If you've watched enough horror movies, you know not to go running off with strangers. I needed answers before I did anything, even if it was just getting dressed and standing up. Looking around for a nurse call button to call for security just in case, I frowned not finding one and felt panic and anger begin to boil up within me. I volunteered as a candy striper for four years in high school and knew hospitals inside and out. This was no hospital. Trying to come up with a reasonable explanation to what was going on I took a deep breath and the air was clean; no bitter antiseptic smell of a hospital. Instead it smelled more like my dad's office with the Clean Linen air fresheners and reed diffusers stuck in corners. Nothing in the room seemed familiar. I hated the feeling of having no idea what was going on.

"Where am I?" I reiterated. Something didn't seem right and my gut was sending warning signals. Everything felt off somehow. If this wasn't a hospital, where exactly was I? Where were my family, doctors, or nurses?

"It's okay, Lucy; we're here to help you. My name's Cassie. You've already met Max, and the other two guys out there are Adam and James. I know you've got a lot of questions, and I'm going to do my best to answer them for you. But first let's get you up and dressed." She reached again to pull me up, but I resisted.

"No!" I yelled, sitting up and bringing my now red face toward her. She smiled sweetly. "I want answers first. What the hell is going on?" That smile didn't fool me. Lots of psychos smile while they plot to kill you. Momma didn't raise no fool. I dug into the bed adamant I wasn't going anywhere and the heart monitors beeped loudly as my pulse raced.

She took a deep breath and gradually released it before speaking. "Okay. I get it. What do you want to know first?"

"Well I know you said your name is Cassie, but that doesn't tell me anything. Who are you people?"

Cassie watched me calmly, and I had to give her some credit. If someone had rudely yelled at me, I would have a few choice words in retort. Cassie didn't even smirk; she just kept smiling sweetly as she twisted a strawberry blonde curl around her finger and sat softly on the foot of the bed.

Her voice remained soothing as she replied, "Well, I'll need to start by explaining what happened to you before we get into who we are. What's the last thing you remember?"

"I remember being in the car with Janice and then a horribly loud sound. Oh my God, Janice! Is she okay? Where is she?"

Cassie nodded, which reassured me momentarily. "Your friend is fine. You were in a car accident. A drunk driver sideswiped your driver side door. Janice survived the accident."

I narrowed my eyes and thought about what she didn't say with that sentence. "Don't you mean *we* survived the accident?"

"No, Lucy," Cassie shook her head hesitantly. "I don't mean that. You didn't physically survive the accident. Your body was killed instantly."

This woman was a few fries short of a happy meal. "What are you talking about? I'm right here! I'm not dead!"

"That's what I'm trying to explain, Lucy. Your body died. But before your spirit went to its destination, you were chosen. It's quite an honor actually; there are only a few of us."

None of her answers made sense, and they were not making me feel any better about allowing her to help me. I was getting tired of her purposely vague answers and was quickly growing irritated. It must have shown on my face because she kept talking.

"We are the Patronus. We help protect the spirits of the departed until a decision has been made about their ultimate destination. You were chosen to join us when you died. We've been waiting for you to make the transition and now that you've finally woken up, we're here to train you for your assignment. Personally, I am super excited you're finally ready. I'm tired of being the only girl on the team and I could really use some girls only time!"

I expected her to smile because this had to be a joke. I was sitting right here, alive. I wasn't a Patronus or whatever she called it. I glanced around for the hidden cameras, certain a microphone was hiding behind an IV pole or cameras were in the large "Exit" sign by the door.

"Ha! Good one. You really had me going for a minute. Now seriously, where is my family? My mom and dad must be freaking out by now. I've gotta let them know I'm okay." I tried to stand up on my own but she placed her hand on my shoulder and firmly pushed me back in the bed.

"I know this is hard for you to believe Lucy. Nowadays humans are taught that anything supernatural is a fairytale and make believe. You need to understand that I'm speaking the truth. The sooner you accept this, the easier it'll be. There are things in this universe that exist even if you don't believe in them. Your life as you knew it is over, but you're still moving forward. Consider yourself blessed; only a few get this opportunity. Would you have rather moved on with no memories at all?"

Her face conveyed no smile, and her tone projected her earnestness. I could see she was taking this seriously, and I stopped for a moment to consider what she was saying. Even as I did, I thought I must be losing it for even considering the possibility that it was true. She stood up and crossed her arms over her chest and took a few steps away from me.

"Lucy, where do you think fairytales come from? Or all of the stories about mythological creatures for that matter? The stories are as old as civilization itself. Many of the things people think of myths today are real, but human understanding is limited." She sighed and adjusted so she was facing me when she spoke. "Humans couldn't believe that we existed, so throughout history humans have made new names for what they couldn't explain. The ancient Greeks thought of us as gods like Hecate, Thanatos, and Iapetos. The Puritans thought of us as witches and many innocent women were burned because of the townspeople who refused to expand their beliefs. Still others thought of us as angels and demons. Today, most people think of us as pretend. But where do you think the idea for all of these creatures, myths, gods, and legends came from? No one's muse is that creative. The Patronus have always been here, guarding over humankind."

Even though I was skeptical, I spoke to her in my most serious tone. "So what you're saying is that angels, witches, and demons all exist? And now I'm one of them?"

"There are things that exist that you've never known. No, you're not an angel or demon. We're a different type of being, for lack of a better word. We are the Patronus. We exist in a separate realm than everything else and are a neutral party. When a person dies their spirit is in peril. There are many factions vying for the right to that spirit. For some, it's an easy choice. If someone has lived a terrible life full of hatred and evil, the decision to send them to the Omega is an easy one. There are some who have lead pure lives, selfless and honorable. The decision for them to go to the Alpha is even easier, but they are the minority. The majority of people are in the muddled middle. They weren't evil, but they made mistakes in their life. They weren't pure, but they tried to do right. For those spirits, there is a fight."

My face must have betrayed my bewilderment because she followed by saying, "Think of it this way: One of these fights is like a battle between two CEOs for the rights to own a new stock that has come on the market. Until a decision has been made, that stock is volatile and needs protection. That's our job. We protect it until an outcome has been reached and the spirit can move on safely."

"And now I'm a Patronus?" She nodded once so I continued, "Why me?"

Cassie didn't answer for a few seconds. Instead, she stared at me as though she was trying to decide how to answer. "When your body died, your spirit was given to us to protect. James, the leader of our division, saw that your spirit was different–special. You had the essence we look for when selecting new members. We then evaluated the short life you led. You helped those who were less fortunate and in need at the local hospital. You showed great leadership as the captain of your swimming team, and you were strong when family needed you in a tough time and selflessly helped them." I glanced down sheepishly and began to blush, but Cassie continued, "You were perfect for this role! James petitioned the Alpha and Omega to give your spirit to us so we could add you to our ranks. They agreed and here you are. We brought you to our facility to transition into your new life."

I studied my body. It still looked as I remembered. I still had the same long, wavy, dark honey colored hair that I'd always had. I still had my long legs and lean frame. I didn't seem any different. "But I'm still me. What transitioned? And what's up with the arm and leg machines?"

"We've given you your body back. When a new Patronus joins us, we've found it helps them feel better about what's happening if they have a sense of familiarity. But since that original body had been dead, we needed to revive it. That's why you're here. It takes a while for the physical transition and since your body was battered in the accident, it took a little longer. The machines keep your body moving and keep the muscles from atrophying while the rest heals. That process is over now and it's time for your training to begin."

"Ew! You dug up my body? That's so gross!" I scanned the room for a mirror, expecting to see something out of *Night of the Living Dead*. Snickers came from outside the door.

"I thought you said you were going to give us some time? Go back to the Commons. We'll meet you there in a little bit!" Cassie yelled to Max, who was apparently standing just outside the doorway.

"Cass, you know I've been waiting for this." Max's voice was so soft I almost missed it.

"I know, but you know rushing things is only going to make it more difficult. Now go!" Cassie ordered, and there was a deep sigh, then footsteps begrudgingly strode away.

"Um, Cassie, what did he mean when he said 'been waiting for this'?" I asked. Maybe I hadn't heard right or he was talking about something else.

"Don't worry about that now. First things first, we need to get you dressed and walking." She hooked her hands under my armpits and pulled me to a standing position, and this time I didn't fight her. I still didn't allow myself to take what she said one hundred percent seriously, but I wasn't afraid she would hurt me either. This was all happening so fast. My head was spinning. I couldn't deal with the idea that I'd died, so I decided to just deal with one thing at a time. My legs felt like I ran a marathon, and I almost fell to the floor. Thankfully, Cassie was still holding on to me so I stayed standing. Well, more like leaning.

"Take it slow; it's been five months since you've last used these legs. It's going to be a while till you've recovered completely." Cassie slowly lowered me back down onto the bed to a sitting position.

My eyes bugged out of my head as I took in what she had said. "Five months?! Are you kidding me?" The shock of it made me glad I was sitting down. Had I really been dead for five months? Lying in this room? Had my parents and friends and family really been mourning me all this time?

"My parents! I have to let them know I'm okay!" I tried to jump up again but was stopped by Cassie.

"No, Lucy, I'm sorry. You're parents can't know about this. They think you're dead and have already mourned your death. It would be cruel to tell them otherwise. Besides, you're not even on earth anymore. You're in our realm now and couldn't see them even if you tried."

I thought about what she said as tears silently streamed down my cheeks. My parents thought I was dead. They had a funeral for me. They must be hurting so badly. And then the realization hit me–I'm never going to see them again. More tears slid down my cheeks but Cassie didn't say anything. She just handed me a tissue and let me cry.

I stayed like that for a good ten minutes, silently crying over my own death. It was a lot to digest. I had a lot of life changing news in the last hour or so. I would never graduate, get married, or have kids. I'd never grow old with the love of my life. I'd never fall in love. I wiped the last of my tears and took a deep breath. Cassie put her arms around me again and helped me into a standing position.

"I know it's a lot to take in, but we're all here to help you. You're one of us now and we're not going to let you deal with this alone." Cassie vowed softly as she helped me into a pair of black yoga pants and a tee shirt.

"I don't get it. If we're in another realm and I'm not even alive, then why do I still feel exactly the same? Why do I feel emotions like pain or excitement?" I thought back to Max running his fingers through my hair and my heart did a little happy dance. Yeah, I was definitely feeling lots of emotions, though normally they weren't this out of control. Maybe it was a side effect of my transition? "Shouldn't I be different somehow?"

She smiled. "But you are different, Lucy. Just not in the ways you're thinking of. We'll explain more later. Some of the changes you'll realize on your own, but for right now we want to take you back to the Dwelling." She opened a drawer and pulled out socks and sneakers. I sat back down to put them on and stood up to face her.

"Okay, now what?"

"Now, we get out of here! I know you don't remember, but I've been here watching you for the last five months and I am thoroughly sick of this place. Let's go home."

As she spoke, a thousand more questions popped into my head. "Home? Dwelling?" I asked, trying to ask the biggest questions first.

"Yes, you'll live with us now. More specifically, with me, as my roommate. But don't worry, most of the time you'll have the place to yourself." She winked at me and gave me a sly look. I remembered her saying she was with Adam, one of the other guys who was in my room when I woke up. Not knowing what to say to that, I just smiled and we stepped out to face my new world.

Two

Once out of the room, I could see it wasn't like a hospital at all. It was a very bright building where light poured in from multiple skylights down the long hallway with many doors on either side. There was nothing in the central area like a nurses' station and no one in uniform walking around. There were a few people going in or out of different rooms or down the hallway with a sense of purpose. Cassie ignored most, but to a few she gave a small nod as we ambled by. The hallway was a lot longer than it looked and I was getting tired fast. I hadn't used my legs in months, so it was taking its toll. I tried not to let it show and keep pace with Cassie, but after about fifty yards she stopped to let me rest. I'd been a college Division One swimmer and was pretty fit, but this short distance made me want to curl up and take a nap.

"Thanks, I can't believe how tired I am." I felt ashamed. I'd worked hard throughout my twenty-two years to stay active and fit. I was never a couch potato and now I could barely walk a few yards without needing a break. Cassie let go of my waist now that I had better balance and turned to look at me.

"Patience. It'll come back to you. You won't need to do much physically for the first training course anyway." I didn't understand what she meant, but I'd already bombarded her with enough questions and let it go for now. We continued through the long corridor and finally came to an oversized set of creamy yellow French doors. They looked like the kind you would see leading to a balcony in a bedroom, but strangely they were in the middle of the hallway.

    Cassie paused for a second and focused on me. "Ready for your new life?" she asked, but didn't wait for my response before ushering me through the doors. Once through we were in another type of room altogether. It reminded me of my college student union with large oversized leather couches scattered around several big screen TVs showing everything from SportsCenter, to CNN and The Simpsons. Across from the TV area stood a few pool and foosball tables with several people immersed in games. In the center of the room separating the areas was a bar (which my college, unfortunately, did not have) and I noticed several sets of eyes turned to check out the new girl. I was glad Cassie hadn't stopped moving because I couldn't shake the feeling of embarrassment at being the center of this attention.

    "Where are we?" I asked as I surveyed my surroundings and took everything in. Just beyond a pool table where a group of guys were playing and eyeing me up and down, we spotted some familiar faces. Max noticed me first, quickly stood up and started toward us. Men who I assumed were Adam and James were engrossed in a game of chess and were unaware of our approach until Cassie cleared her throat. They jumped up, startled, and quickly stood up grabbing more seats to add for Cassie and me.

    "This is the Commons," Cassie answered. "It's a place for us to relax or unwind or just wait sometimes. It's used by all the Patroni in our division."

    "And how many are in our division?" My curiosity about everything stirred up hundreds of questions in my mind. While rationally I knew I should still be skeptical, I suddenly had the urge to know everything about this new world.

"About 300 give or take." Max's deep, smoldering voice gave me goose bumps. I shivered slightly at the sight of him, hoping he didn't notice. He had this unprecedented affect from the first words he spoke to me, and I wasn't quite sure what to make of it. His arm took the place of Cassie's around my waist as he helped me towards the chairs where the guys were sitting. I instantly relaxed against him and felt calm. He found a black leather club chair and carefully eased me down into it. I thanked him and he sat down in the chair next to me. He reached out his arm as if to touch me, but paused. My body urged me to reach for him, but I didn't. The look on his face told me he had the same thought, but he quickly pulled his arm back and set his hands in his lap. The other two men just smiled at each other. Cassie took a seat next to who I assumed was Adam and snuggled against him. He kissed her forehead and she beamed up at him.

"I guess we should formally introduce ourselves." Proclaimed the man who by process of elimination had to be James. "I'm James, and I'm the leader of our division."

I admired him more closely. He was tall as well, but not as tall as Max. With straight sandy blonde hair worn to the tips of his ears and green eyes, he reminded me of a devilishly handsome surfer. A small half inch scar ran down his left temple that enhanced the features of his face rather than detracting from its beauty. It made me want to trace my finger down it to make sure he was okay. His body was just as yummy as his face with broad shoulders, sculpted arms and a narrow waist. I put him in his upper twenties, and damn if he wasn't fine. Women must fawn all over him.

"This is Adam, and you've already met Cassie," James continued.

Adam nodded at me. He was about six foot and had long brown hair to his shoulders that he kept tied back in a loose ponytail. He had the physique of a football player and was by far the biggest guy in the bunch. His neck was thicker than my calf and all I could see through his tight grey tee shirt were muscles. Cassie had good taste.

"And finally, Max, the miscreant of our crew," James said with a chuckle and a wink to Max. Max threw a pillow at him and flipped him the finger.

"Thanks for the great introduction, asshole!" Max teased. James threw the pillow back and laughed.

"Hi Lucy," Max said, looking at me again. He smiled as he said my name, and I could see the deep dimple in his cheek again.

As I finally got a chance to really look at him, I had to admit he was by far the most attractive man I'd ever seen in real life. Being tall, I was always attracted to bigger guys. When he helped me to my seat, I couldn't help but notice he towered over me, which wasn't easy to do. He wasn't as broad as Adam, but definitely had an amazing physique with broad, defined arms, shoulders, and chest leading to strong muscular legs. My stomach did flip flops, and I fought the urge to touch him just to see if he was real. I had never felt so instantly attracted to another person. The force of it was so strong–like gravity was pulling me towards him. I wondered if he could see me blushing while I assessed him and quickly stared down at my feet embarrassed. He never looked away and kept smiling.

"Hi everyone," I murmured, my voice just above a whisper. It's funny, in most circumstances I was the least shy person in a room, but surrounded by all these gorgeous people, I suddenly felt self-conscious. It was obvious I was the youngest one in the group and that thought made me nervous. I sat there absorbing everything around, but the silence was killing me. I racked my brain for a witty comment to fill the void, but my mind was suddenly blank. James spoke first.

"I hope Cassie did some of the initial explaining for you, and I'm sure you still have a million questions. Being the leader of this division, feel free to come to me with anything you need to know, but really, any of us can probably answer your questions. We'll give you the day to settle in, and tomorrow begin the formal training for your new role."

"Not a whole lot of adjustment time to this new life. That's okay though, I'm anxious to learn what this is all about," I addressed the group, eager to jump in and get started.

"Wow, we honestly didn't expect you to be this gung ho," Max commented, clearly surprised at my answer. "How about a tour first and then I'll show you to the Dwellings?"

The thought of Max and me in my bedroom sent a shiver down my spine for the third time in as many hours. He put his hand on me. "Are you okay? Cold?" he asked, most likely concerned that I hadn't yet recovered from my transition. Now I was sure I had just turned three shades of red. This was so unlike me! I never acted this way around guys. Maybe it was residual effects from the transition or something. I made a mental note to ask Cassie about it later.

"Oh, um, I'm fine." I stammered, trying to brush off his concern. I stood up as he did and he placed his hand on the small of my back, leading me away from the group. With his hand there, my whole body became warm and I couldn't help but smile. I would walk with him for miles just to keep his hand on me.

He led me through the Commons, introducing me to a few people in other divisions. I smiled as they introduced themselves and made small talk, telling me how much fun I would have and making promises to get together for dinner real soon. He showed me a dining facility with buffet style service that was apparently open 24 hours a day and had a small coffeehouse attached. I sighed happily, for nothing could be too bad as long as I had a good Quad Venti Nonfat Café Mocha available. Next, he pointed out what appeared to be a small reading room filled with thousands of books and DVDs on bookshelves from floor to ceiling. I traced my fingers along their worn leather spines and breathed in their scent. There was nothing quite like the smell of a good book. We eventually entered yet another room with all types of art supplies whether you wanted to draw, paint, or even mold clay.

As we continued the tour, he leaned over to whisper to me, "It's not all work, we have lots of time to have fun." I instantly blushed as I thought of fun activities I'd like to do with Max in private. What had gotten into me? I'd never acted this way before! I really needed to snap out of it before I made a total ass out of myself.

"The Commons has lots of things to do when we're not busy protecting a spirit," he continued, pointing to another small room where six people were playing board games.

"Okay, let me see if I've got this straight. We're no longer human," I started.

"Correct."

"But we can still eat, sleep, watch TV, and have to work?" I questioned. "Do we get paid?"

"No, we don't get paychecks because there's no need for money here. We never go without and are given what we need or want within reason. And yes, we can still eat, sleep, and watch TV. You need to remember we were all human once. It's in our comfort zone to continue to do these things. We don't need much food or sleep to sustain us, but we still enjoy those things. We only take small naps rather than sleeping eight hours or more a night."

"And how long have you worked here?" I asked, curious to learn more about his life.

"About 135 years," he replied. "I was one of the newest additions to the team before you came along."

"135 years!" I gasped. "You've been here that long? How long do we live?"

"We can live forever. But there are a few things that can kill us, like decapitation, having our hearts impaled, or having our blood drained from us. On the plus side, we never get sick, and we heal rapidly from most injuries. We will exist here forever and not move on from this realm. We don't go to the Alpha or the Omega or any of the others vying for spirits." He shrugged.

"Am I to assume the Alpha and Omega is God and Satan? And who are the others?" We stopped by a room with stoves, sinks, refrigerators and long, black marble counters. I assumed it was for people who enjoyed cooking, but now it stood empty. He leaned against the wall as if considering how to respond and we stood for a minute in silence.

"You can think of them in those terms. They've been called lots of things throughout time. We've also been called lots of things: guardian angels, fairies, saints, ghosts, even aliens! And our realm has been called many things: heaven, purgatory, limbo, or another dimension. But those are just different terms for the same things. I'm not sure how much Cassie already explained to you, but let me try to expound. Modern religions teach that everything is good or evil, but in reality there are many shades of gray. Life's complicated, and people are forced to make complicated decisions. After they die things don't suddenly become black and white. There are as many options as shades of gray. Some get punished for things they've done, some get rewarded for work they've done. Some, like kids, don't get either and just get a second chance by being reborn. But no matter what choice is made, we protect them from all sides until there is decision."

"What do they need protecting from?" I asked, suddenly interested in the whole idea.

"Sometimes we protect them from themselves. Dying can be traumatic and some don't react well. Mostly we protect them from having their spirit stolen," he explained. "There are certain entities out there who don't wish to wait and do things fairly. They just want to collect as many spirits as they can to build their numbers. These are the 'others' that I told you about. Entities that are dying out and will do anything to keep from going extinct. Werewolves, vampires, and fairies– things like that," he remarked with a straight face.

"You've got to be kidding me!" I cried, my jaw practically dropping to the floor. I was astonished that he was so serious. "Are you telling me that we're protecting spirits from becoming supernatural creatures like vampires and werewolves?"

"Yep. Among other things." He had a straight face and a serious expression.

It took a minute for that to sink in. "I thought a vampire or werewolf had to bite a person in order to change them, and that's if you believe that they even exist."

"Many of the legends that have been passed down are purposefully false. They started those myths to protect their true identities. Werewolves don't scratch or bite humans, vampires aren't allergic to garlic. Those are just made up stories so no one suspects who they truly are. In reality, both create new beings by stealing spirits before they've been assigned to their final destination. Our job is to make sure that doesn't happen." I leaned against a wall, putting my hands in my pockets as I took a minute for his words to sink in.

"So vampires and werewolves steal a bunch of old people who die? That seems an odd choice."

"It doesn't matter how old or young they are, the vampires are just in it for the soul. Once they have it, they can give it any form they choose. The very old and very young are often the easiest targets. The little ones haven't had enough experience and don't know to be weary."

"But millions of people die every day, how do we protect them all?" I asked.

"We have resources available that allow us to shield spirits from view and after their passing, they move into our realm where it's harder for people to break in. We guard them until a decision has been made. The problem arises when a spirit gets nervous and tries to run away without waiting. In some instances, they wander off outside of our protection. Most of the time though the Weres and Vamps will find them all on their own by sneaking in during a spirits arrival or snatching them before they make it here."

"Where would these spirits run to? Or why would they run, especially if it's dangerous," I interrupted. We started walking again, and his hand returned to the small of my back. It made my heart want to burst forth from my chest with excitement, but I kept my face calm.

"Many of them try to go back home, or to the Alpha or Omega to beg for mercy. There are doors in our realm that take you to these places. Some spirits are disgruntled and easy to take because they don't want to be dead. The bloodsuckers offer them life after death, one where you can go home. The problem is, once they take on the vampire form, they don't want what they once had. They want blood. They want to control life, not be a part of it. That is why we need to protect the souls. If they leave this realm, that's when they're most susceptible and they need the most protection. That's when we end up fighting."

"I see." I nodded pensively. "Is it dangerous?"

"It can be, but we'll train you how to fight and protect." He stopped and led me through another set of French doors into what appeared to be dorm rooms. I peered inside a few of the open rooms and to my amazement, they didn't resemble like dorms at all. They reminded me of the large luxury apartments that you might find in New York City or something.

"Okay, enough business." I put my hand to his chest to get him to stop. Solid and sculpted, it felt like steel beneath my hand. I let out a breath in appreciation. Mustering up my courage I said, "Tell me more about you."

He turned his gaze from mine, and for the first time he didn't look completely confident. He had a hint of vulnerability in his eyes. I absently wondered why talking about his personal life would bother him, and I hoped he didn't have a horrible or violent death– or even worse, a wife. It might break my heart in two to hear that he'd loved another woman. That he still thought about her or pined for her still. Why does that bother me? I barely know him! I must still be loopy from the drugs at the medical area.

"There's not much to tell," he confessed, shuffling his feet. What was making him nervous? Oh, God! It was a wife. Well, crap on a cracker! That sucked big time.

"Oh come on, there's got to be *something* to tell me." Urging him to continue I asked, "Where did you live before you died? What did you do for a living?" I purposefully avoided anything about his love life at all.

"I was a teacher. A professor actually. I taught anthropology at Florida State University. That's where I lived."

Phew! Not where "we" lived which made the knot in my stomach loosen up a bit. "Oh wow! You look so young! Way too young to be a professor."

"It was a different time, and I completed my studies earlier than most. I finished secondary school at sixteen and finished University by twenty. I was lucky enough to receive a grant to continue my education and was working on my PhD while teaching."

"That's," I paused, thinking of the right words, "really impressive. When did you teach there?" I really wanted to know more about him, but I knew that he was uncomfortable and was trying to bring up the subject gradually.

"I became a professor in 1877 when I was twenty-two, just a few years after the University opened. I taught for a year and a half before I died."

I paused, waiting for him to continue but he didn't. "Is your death too painful to talk about?" I asked, feeling slimy for prying when I knew he didn't want to talk, but and I had to know more. I just wouldn't–or couldn't–let it go.

He didn't answer me right away; he stared at me like he was looking directly at my soul. I stopped breathing for a second and stared back. His gaze didn't leave my eyes, and I silently prayed it never would. I had never in all my life felt anything like it. Being trapped in his eyes was the most wonderful feeling I've ever experienced. It felt like absolutely nothing was or could ever be wrong with the world. I wasn't sure how long we stood like that, but it didn't matter. It felt surreal to feel so connected to someone I'd only just met, but the feelings were so intense, I was unable to question them.

After what could have been years, he began speaking again. "My death is still a sore spot for me. I know everyone has a story and I should just get over it, but it's still a little raw, even after all these years. I'll tell you about it someday. And I'm sure you'll be hearing plenty of 'my death was worse than your death' stories after you've been here long enough. Find David Stone, his death is wild!"

I nodded quickly, embarrassed by my brash behavior. "Oh, of course. I'm sorry to pry. I shouldn't have asked."

"Please don't worry, I didn't take offense. But I will tell you this, I had an amazing life. I loved everything about it and leaving it and accepting that I couldn't change things was really hard. I love being a Patronus now, but for many years, if given the choice, I would have gone back." He stopped talking for a moment and placed his hand on the small of my back, indicating that we should continue walking and led me to an elevator which we rode to the third floor. "But things are different now. I am happy and things are working out well with my afterlife."

"So teaching was that great? I always gave my teachers some grief –turning in papers late or making smart remarks in class. My teachers were always calling home and telling my parents what a pain in the ass I was. My guidance counselor told me once I didn't need a second language because I was already fluent in English and Sarcasm! I was just too stubborn for my own good. College was great though. I wish I could have finished. I was just about to graduate when I died."

"They awarded you your degree posthumously. I checked while you were still transitioning," Max announced.

"Oh wow, awesome! Gee, I hope they didn't try to stick Mom and Dad with the bill. How much would that suck having to pay for your dead daughter's degree that she couldn't even use!" I awkwardly teased.

"I'm pretty sure they make allowances for these kinds of things," Max chuckled. His smile should be bottled and given as a substitute for Prozac. We stopped outside a door marked 316. He moved his hand from my back and slid it against my waist, then down my arm until he was holding my hand lightly.

"Here we are," he announced. "This is your and Cassie's Dwelling. She's been looking forward to getting a roommate for, oh, at least fifty years, so I know you'll get along just fine. I'm in room 490 upstairs if you need anything." He paused for a second and just studied me. I thought he was contemplating kissing me and I felt my eyes involuntarily slide closed in anticipation. After a moment, I opened them realizing I wasn't being kissed and internally pouted. When I glanced up at him, he was staring at me with those smoldering eyes and my hand was still firmly clasped in his. I felt embarrassed, again, but he was smiling.

"I may be biased," he started, "but I think being a Patronus is one of the best things that can happen to you once you die. We live very similarly to our previous lives –we can laugh, play, and even," he paused, gazing deep in my eyes, "love."

I stretched up on my tip toes as if in invitation to kiss me, something I've never wanted so badly in my entire existence when I heard him clear his throat and continue. "I mean look at Cassie and Adam, they're the perfect couple."

I blinked, realizing I'd probably just made a fool of myself when Cassie opened the door I was leaning against, and I started to fall through. I stumbled and caught myself before smashing onto the floor. Nope, *now* I've made a complete fool of myself. Cassie and Max both gasped and reached out to steady me. I could see Cassie biting her cheek to keep from laughing.

"There you are!" she greeted, visibly swallowing her laugh. "I was beginning to think that Max was trying to keep you all to himself." She smiled up at Max, her smile containing a secret. He quickly turned his gaze and I wondered what it was all about.

"I guess this is goodnight." Max sighed reluctantly while giving Cassie the evil eye. "I'll see you tomorrow. Sleep well," he said, momentarily hesitating to catch my eye for one more second before he turned and strode away.

Cassie beamed as she took my hand and led me through the Dwelling, giving me the grand tour. It was bigger and more modern than what I was expecting and we each had our own bedroom and bathroom. There was a little sitting area with a small TV and two ultra suede loveseats. The walls were painted a deep blue with a white chair rail and wainscoting on the bottom. Several large paintings of seaside landscapes hung on the walls and the pub table and chairs in the eat-in kitchen held tropical themed knick knacks reminding me of many of the vacation beach condos by my home. It made me smile that there was a sense of familiarity to this place and that's what I needed after such a tumultuous day. It was quant and homey, but not as roomy as I expected. As if seeing my question, Cassie said, "It's smaller than a normal living and dining room, but we don't use it very much. We mostly hang out and eat in the Commons. This area is mostly used just to grab a quick snack or to relax with a bit of privacy."

I nodded, and she continued leading me to the bedroom. I was taken aback when I realized many of my things were already in it. The room was almost an exact replica of the one at my parents' house. In it were my sheets and comforter from home and my desk, complete with laptop and bankers lamp. When I opened the closet, my entire wardrobe was already hung up like I'd been living there for years.

"How did you get this all here?" I asked.

Cassie just winked and plopped down on the bed sitting Indian style. "So, how are you doing so far with everything? Have we completely overwhelmed you yet?"

I didn't answer right away, continuing to survey my room. Nothing had changed, but everything had changed. So much of it reminded me of home I almost forgot what happened to me. It was a very strange sensation to be surrounded by things that held so many memories for me and brought me so much comfort, but at the same time, I knew nothing was normal anymore and the comforts of my old life were gone forever. I couldn't open the door to this bedroom and step across the hallway into my parents' room or open the window beside my desk and see the old dogwood tree blooming outside. Or climb down the tree to sneak off and lie on the beach with Tommy McDunn at 2:00 AM to watch the stars.

I glanced back over at Cassie. She was peering at the photographs on my vanity mirror from high school. I smiled and pointed to one of the pictures. "That's my little sister Jessica," I explained. "I'm really worried about her now that I'm not there. She has leukemia. It was in remission when I last spoke with her, but now I won't be around to make sure she's okay or help her with her homework, or teach her the breaststroke."

"Were you close?" Cassie asked.

"Extremely. Even though we weren't close in age, she was my best friend. She always wanted to do everything I did." I smiled, remembering her sitting next to me at my vanity when she was five mimicking me as I put on makeup and getting it all over.

"When she got sick, she never cried if I was there with her. She told my mom she wanted to be strong for me. She is the bravest person I've ever met." I thought about crying again, but then I remembered what my mom always said: "Are you going to react or are you going to act? You're not a bystander in your life. You're in the driver's seat so step on the pedal already!" Crying about it wouldn't help. I needed to suck it up and decide where to steer the next course in my life.

"Trust me when I tell you I'm speaking from experience–life is not fair. Nothing about it is. But here, in this realm, we can make sure that every spirit gets a fair shot at moving on. We can protect them from having that opportunity stolen. The werewolves and especially the vampires that try to steal their spirits before they're judged don't care who they are and what they've done in their lives. They don't care what they deserve. They just want to increase their numbers so they don't go extinct. We're doing a really good thing with our afterlife. We're helping too, just in a different way."

I thought about what she said and realized she was right. Helping people shouldn't be restricted to just the people you know. We should want to help all people: family, friend or stranger. I smiled. I decided having her as my roommate was going to make this transition a lot easier. Suddenly, another big question popped into my head.

"Why are the vampire and werewolf populations dying off? People don't know about them, so shouldn't they be safe?" I asked.

"You'll learn more about this tomorrow from James, but let me give you the basics. To make a long story short: Vampires have existed for almost as long as humankind. They are a result of the evolutionary process gone wrong. They've passed their existence in the shadows, living on the fringes of society. But modern blood-borne diseases like malaria, HIV, and some cancers have caused them to sicken and die when they would feed on infected people. Humans can go and get vaccinations and treatments. Vampires, not so much. And while a vampire can live for an extended period of time, they aren't immortal. They couldn't fight off these diseases and quickly started succumbing to them." I nodded in understanding and she continued.

"Human diseases caused several thousand vampires to die– think Spanish Flu and Black plague. Those were cover ups for the sudden deaths of many sick supernatural creatures. Years ago, if too many humans resided close by the vamps would just pack up and move to a new sparsely populated or deserted area. Now with global overpopulation there aren't a whole lot of areas that they can go to get away from humans. Without deserted areas to stay, exposure became a problem.

With the advent of blood banks, vampires can get nourishment much easier, but they still don't fit in with modern societies too well. Pop culture became obsessed with the supernatural and stories of their existence spread. While most people still thought of them as fictitious, many sought them out either to be a groupie or kill them. The times when their existence was kept secret were quickly passing and they rapidly went from the thousands to the hundreds. They are freaking out that the entire species is going to die off, so they've been stealing more and more spirits and converting them in an attempt to increase their numbers."

"So that's why more Patroni are needed?" I questioned. "To keep the spirits from becoming remade into a vampire or werewolf?"

"In a nutshell," she asserted very matter-of-factly.

"What about other parts of the legend? Living in coffins, turning into bats, and only coming out at night? Are those part myth or real?" I continued with my barrage of questions.

"Ha! Myth."

"But they drink blood?"

"Vampires do require blood as part of their nourishment but it doesn't have to be human blood. Animal blood works just as well, which is why they like to live apart from the humans. They don't need them and they can avoid exposure. Of course, they don't prefer animal blood, but if it's that or exposure and a possible illness, they'll take the animal blood.

But enough about that, let's talk about the good stuff," she broke in, abruptly changing topics. "What do you think of Max?" She was almost squealing in excitement, and my face instantly flushed.

"Um, he's nice," I remarked shyly, fidgeting with the fringe of the quilt my grandmother had made me that covered my bed.

"Oh come on! You've got to give me more than that! I was watching you with him tonight and I'm watching your face right now. You're blushing! You can give me a little more than 'he's nice'."

I took a deep breath. I hadn't even had time to analyze my own feelings about him yet, or why in the world I was so instantly and increasingly attracted to him but Cassie wanted me to give her all the juicy details. "Well," I began, "he seems like a great guy. And he is pretty cute...okay really freakin' hot. I can't seem to stop thinking about him. I've only known him a few hours and I am acting like an idiot around him." I finally admitted. She opened her mouth to say something but I kept talking before she had a chance to speak. "While we're on the topic, what did he mean when he said he'd been waiting for me? It sounded like he meant longer than the five months it took me to wake up."

"Lucy, I'm sorry. I wish I could tell you, but it's just not my story to tell. Plus, I really think you'd rather hear that from him," she surmised, telling me absolutely nothing but spiking my curiosity like it was a match to a pile of flint.

"You've got to give me something to go on! Come on Cassie, *anything*," I begged.

"All right, but here's all I'll say. I think you find him more than just attractive. I think you already genuinely care for him. You have no idea why since you've only just met him and it's freaking you out."

My mouth dropped open. I couldn't think of anything to say, it was like she had pulled the words directly from my head. She continued, "I think you should spend some time with him. I'm pretty sure he'd really like that too." She had a sly smile on her face as she shuffled off my bed and headed towards the door.

Standing at the edge of my room she said, "You should probably rest now. It's been a long day and we have an even longer one tomorrow. Sleep well!"

With that, she strode out of the bedroom and closed the door behind her. As if she'd placed the idea in my head, suddenly I felt exhausted and couldn't wait until my head hit the pillow.

Three

I slept like the dead. I yawned and stretched, rolling over in my bed and chuckling as I realized the pun I'd made. I loved being wrapped up all warm and cozy in the comfort of my blankets. They still smelled like home and I didn't want to get out of bed. I closed my eyes for a few more seconds, beginning to daydream about Max. He was beside me, wrapping me in his strong arms, nuzzling and placing tiny baby kisses along my neck, down to my ear, and across my jaw. I leaned into him taking in the aroma of his spicy aftershave, gingerly placing my lips against his. I turned to face him, meeting his eyes and refusing to look away. I could get lost in those baby blues for days. I parted my lips slightly in invitation for him to kiss me. As I felt his soft, moist tongue finally make contact with mine—the toilet flushed. I opened my eyes, drawn out of my daydream, and sighed. "Always in my dreams, never the man of them," I muttered to myself and threw the covers off, wrapped my robe around me, and trudged out of my bedroom. I had no idea how long I'd slept because I couldn't find a clock anywhere. Cassie was already out in the living room area of our Dwelling sitting on the small loveseat, dressed and ready to go.

"Morning sleepyhead!" she teased as I shuffled into the kitchenette in search of coffee. "Don't worry, you'll need less sleep once you've been at this for a while."

"How long did I sleep?" I inquired, rubbing the sleep from my eyes. I felt like I'd been out for days.

"Almost five hours. You might want to get ready, James will be expecting us." She put down her coffee mug and pulled open a book she was reading. Realizing it was too late to have my morning coffee (going without was equivalent to Chinese water boarding) I stumbled back into my bathroom, found my necessary toiletries, and jumped into the shower. Twenty minutes later, I was ready to go in another pair of yoga pants and a pink racerback tank top. Cassie handed me a to-go coffee cup as we walked out the door. I inhaled its delicious aroma and I could have kissed her for thinking of me. Taking a careful sip and feeling its sweet, warm healing powers slide down my throat, I thanked her repeatedly. It was exactly how I took it, sweet with sugar, and I wondered absently how she knew.

"No problem," she replied, "I can't live without my morning fix either. And trust me–you're going to need it. You've got a long day ahead preparing for your new life."

"What exactly am I doing today?" I asked, anxious to get started.

"Honestly, I don't know. It's been so long since my training sessions I'm not sure what James has in store for you. All I really remember about training is I was exhausted the whole time. But my death was more gruesome than yours so I had a lot more to recover from."

I suspected she was lying, because honestly, who didn't remember their first day in a brand new world? Hell, I remembered my first day of college better than I remembered my last birthday! What she was keeping from me? I dismissed the thought; she must have a good reason. She'd been so open an honest since I first woke up, I would trust her here. Instead, I went a different route in my questioning.

"How did you die?" I inquired shyly. I didn't want to be *that* girl, who asked inappropriate private questions to people they just met, but curiosity was getting the best of me.

She just shrugged and said in a very blasé tone, "I was mauled by a bear while camping," like she was telling me to switch a load of laundry. I stopped in my tracks and gawked at her.

"Come again?" I stammered incredulously.

"My husband and I were camping in the Great Smokies on vacation. I'm originally from Florida like you, but we'd inherited some money from a great aunt who'd died, so we finally took the honeymoon we never had. I had no interest in camping and would have much rather gone to a nice resort in Cuba where I could sunbathe all day, but Matthew would hear none of it. He wanted adventure and to see the mountains since we didn't have any where we lived. I didn't argue and gave in to what he wanted. It didn't really matter what I wanted at that time. On our second day there I was killed." She told me and nudged me to keep moving.

"Oh my God! Are you okay?" I asked, then shook my head as I realized how ridiculous I sounded. Of course she wasn't okay, she died!

Cassie just smiled at me and said, "It was a lifetime ago and I'm a completely different person now. I'm not upset about it anymore. I'm happy with what I was chosen to be, and I'm even happier I found Adam."

"You were married?"

"Yes, I was. For a whole seven months. It was a boy my parents approved of and who had a good standing in society, so I said yes. Things were done differently then, girls didn't get much choice in the matter. My mother told me I'd grow to love him, but I never got the chance."

"You married someone you didn't even love? I can't even imagine a world like that."

Cassie laughed. "Ah, the youth of today, so self-absorbed." I thought about taking offence, but Cassie winked at me and I knew she was just teasing (even if she meant her words). She continued, "Marriage was never about love–it was about property. I needed to keep my family's reputation and marry into a family whose social standing was strong in our community. My father made the decision for me when I was sixteen. I was just lucky enough to get him to agree to push it back a year so I could finish my education. I knew the only way I could really get anywhere in life was by being educated. A good husband can only take you to bed. A good mind can take you anywhere."

I considered her words as we reached the doors that led out of the Dwellings. I didn't quite know what to think about a marriage without love, but I liked that she wasn't going to let her father's decisions or even her own death define her. We left the Dwellings area and passed through the French doors to enter the Commons. It was relatively empty this morning except for a few stragglers inhaling their breakfast, and I realized just how late we were. Just outside, standing in the sunshine, James, Adam and Max were waiting for us. Max smiled as he saw me and I couldn't help but smile back, remembering my daydream from earlier. I felt my cheeks getting hot and tried to think of anything else but him. Of course, that was impossible and my cheeks just grew hotter.

"Ready for today?" he asked as he twisted the gold bracelet that adorned his wrist anxiously. I nodded in reply, too afraid of what might slip out of my mouth to actually speak and I gulped down more coffee. "Good," he replied. "It's going to be a long day."

I glanced at him again and realized his eyes never left my face. I forgot about everything around me as I stared back into his eyes. The crystal clear blue reminded me of how the ice from the glaciers of Alaska looked in the movies. It was a stunning contrast to his jet black hair. It was such a beautiful sight, I wanted to take him by the hand and lead him back to my bedroom so I could make my daydream a reality. Why did I feel this strongly about him? I felt like a twelve year old with her first crush. I really need to snap out of this!

James cleared his throat loudly in an obvious attempt to get our attention and I was instantly reminded that I wasn't *actually* standing alone with Max. "I take it you slept well and are feeling better today?" James inquired. I nodded and he continued, "We're going to start you out with lectures and history lessons about who we are and what we do until your body is fully recovered. Then, in about a week, we'll get you out in the field to shadow some of the team members."

I groaned slightly and got snickers from both Adam and Cassie, who were holding hands as we walked from the Commons to the two story white brick building across the courtyard. "Lectures all day? I'm feeling a thousand times better. Can't I do *something* active? " I begged like a child asking for five more minutes before bedtime. I'd been cooped up and strapped to a bed for months and now free from those bonds, I wanted to try out my new body.

I'd always loved school, but with Max near me, I knew my concentration level wasn't going to be great, especially for listening and paying attention to a lecture. I needed to do something physical to release the nervous energy I'd built up. Then again, this lecture was sure to provide all of the answers I'd been craving. It could hold all of the secrets to life and death.

I perked up at that thought and practically skipped to the lecture hall. Our group strolled through a set of large blue doors and I found what looked like a college classroom complete with long wood tables, three tiered rows of seats and a whiteboard in the front. A projector hung from the ceiling and I half expected to see a PowerPoint presentation like in so many of my college classes. I sat at a table in the front row and watched Cassie and Adam chose one in the back. Max slipped into the seat next to me and before I could drift off into another sexy daydream, I realized with increasing embarrassment that I didn't have a pen and paper with me.

"Do I need to take notes?" I anxiously asked James, unsure of what exactly was expected of me.

"No need for notes, your brain is no longer operating in the same small capacity that it did while you were alive.

You're now close to full brain capacity as a Patronus so you'll find you're able to retain everything I talk about today without writing it down or studying it."

"Where was this extra brain power during college?" I joked. "Think about all the frat parties I wouldn't have had to skip if this had been available! That's a lot of rum and cokes I missed out on."

James chastised me with his glare. For someone so young, he had the authoritative stare down cold. I forced myself to stop smiling, bit the inside of my cheek, and looked serious again. James was a tough nut to crack. He seemed to joke around with the others, but today he was acting like a drill sergeant. I made a mental note to ask Cassie what his deal was when we got back to our Dwelling.

"Actually, our enhanced brain power is the key to a lot of what we're able to do now. It will help you not only retain information, but to control much of what we do as Patroni. It will provide you all the tools necessary to protect, defend, and attack. Think of your brain as a giant computer that just downloaded a ton of new software updates. You went from a Commodore 64 to the iPad 3rd generation," James explained. I brought my hand to the side of my head, awed by his statement. "I've asked the others in your squad here today to help you with any questions you may have. Feel free to interrupt with any questions as we talk. It's been a long time since I was walking the earth, so I don't have quite the same perspective."

"How long have you been a Patronus?" I asked.

"Almost 700 years," he replied. Max chuckled softly when my jaw hit the floor.

"Wow, that's a really long time. You must be an expert at this." I said, trying to wrap my head around the idea of being around for that many years.

With a small smile, James replied, "Oh trust me, there are many here who are much older. I just happen to be the oldest in this unit. But that's not important. Now–let's get started with what you'll actually *need* to know.

The Patroni started out as guardian angels. This was before threats evolved to where they are now and factions started stealing souls. We simply used angels to keep the spirits corralled until it was time for them to move on. It was a lower level job for an angel and was often boring."

"Think of it like a cop stuck at a desk job instead of out on a beat," Cassie interceded. She opened her mouth wide to say something else, but James gave her a look, letting her know he didn't like being interrupted no matter how well meaning. Her mouth reluctantly closed and she lowered her eyes in apology.

"When the world started with the original couple, these guardian angels actually stayed on earth. There was no need for a separate realm. But humanity quickly populated the earth, and a move to this realm was necessary. Then, the evolutionary process started. A sickness would mutate a gene. A plant eaten during gestation would damage DNA. The changing environment would force cells to adapt. Before long, the evolutionary process was in spiral, and enemies were created. And with each new generation, they became more demented and evil than the last. The need for blood warped their sense of humanity. Even Solomon wrote about the early vampires in the Book of Proverbs 30:14."

"There are those whose teeth are swords, whose fangs are knives, to devour the poor from off the earth, the needy from among mankind." Adam recited the verse quietly. I was thrown for a second at the sound of his voice and I realized it was the first time I'd actually heard him speak. He had a soft, Southern drawl that rolled off his tongue like molasses when he spoke and was very pleasing to the ear. It wasn't pronounced enough to make him sound like a hick, but was easy and smooth enough to make it endearing– and sexy. James didn't scold him, but continued.

"Job also mentions them in chapter 29, verse 17. It wasn't until the Puritans came that they were shunned from culture and their existence became a fairytale."

"Wait a minute, I went to church my whole life and to catechism classes and I don't ever remember hearing about vampires in the Bible." I crossed my arms skeptically.

"No, you wouldn't. The Catholic church swept their existence under the rug many moons ago and now explains those verses as hyperbole," Max answered me. "It wasn't a story they wanted leaked."

"And as enemies grew in number, so too did our forces. Our role changed from that of a desk job to one of active warrior. Both the Alpha and Omega wanted to see to it that the balance of the universe was not tipped one way or the other." James stood up and walked to the wall where he crossed his arms and feet at the ankles, getting himself comfortable to dive into more of the story.

Over the next three hours, James taught me a lot about the world that I never knew existed and about the role of the Patroni in the grand scheme of the universe. While I'd only seen a few people hanging out in the Commons last night, I discovered that there were actually about 300 in my division and more than 60 divisions that covered the United States alone.

"It's like US states and territories," Adam said from behind me. "We're divided essentially the same way with a few more divisions in the larger states like Texas and California or in areas where death is more common like inner cities or popular retirement destinations. If a spirit dies in the area of our division, we're responsible for it until a decision's been made."

"What part of the US are we in charge of?" I asked the group.

Max replied, "We cover the same area that you, and actually all of us, lived in when we were alive. We cover Florida."

"But Florida has so many old people in it! Trust me, I'm *always* stuck driving behind them. We must be swamped with business!" I exclaimed, thinking back to all of the elderly people in my parents' neighborhood.

Cassie and Max actually laughed out loud and even James chuckled. "Yes, there are more deaths here than, in say, Rhode Island. But we have more Units to compensate for that fact." James explained to me. "The tricky part is the longer the person's life, the longer it can take to make a decision. They've had more experiences than others so the debate can be longer. Consequently, they're in danger for a longer period of time."

"Okay, well what if you don't die by your house. What happens to a person then? If I'd been going up to Georgia rather than the beach, would I even be here now?"

Cassie took this one, "Well remember what I told you about my death? I died on vacation! But I still ended up in the Florida division near my home. It's about where you lived, not where you died."

"Hmm. I feel bad for gypsies! And what about those people who ride around in their RVs all year? Or snowbirds?"

"There are a few exceptions for more important jobs, but for the most part it's simple. I think you're putting too much thought into this Lucy," Adam chuckled. "Don't over-think it!"

Just as he opened his mouth to say something else, a young woman rushed through the door frantically searching the room. "James! We have a breech. A vampire snuck through one of the doorways attached to a new arrival. You guys are needed STAT!"

James, Max, Adam, and Cassie all jumped up and pressed down on the identical bracelet they were all wearing. I glanced down at my wrist and realized I had the same thick, brushed gold colored bracelet on. It resembled a Roman arm cuff and was about three inches wide all the way around. I didn't see a clasp to take it off and I couldn't find any of the buttons that they seemed to be pressing. "Um, someone wanna fill me in?" I asked, feeling completely lost.

Nobody looked up from what they were doing or answered my question. Baffled, I stared down again at the bracelet and began tapping on random spots, hoping something would happen. As I did, I could see green symbols and letters appear in my peripheral vision. When I searched for the source, I realized it was coming from my eyeball itself. This must have been part of the enhanced brain power. I pushed again on the bracelet and a command screen like on my home computer was visible. I stared at the bracelet. There was no keyboard, so how was I supposed to work it?

Cassie giggled for a second reading the confusion on my face and said, "Magic!"

I was getting frustrated both at myself for not figuring it out and with everyone around me keeping me in the dark. They all appeared ready to go and suddenly I felt very out of place. What was I supposed to do? I looked over at Max and he must have had the same question. He shouted at James, "You guys go ahead. I'll bring Lucy back to the Commons and meet up with you."

"Yes, that's a good idea James." Cassie chimed in, bouncing slightly on the balls of her feet with excitement, or maybe it was nervous apprehension.

"No, it's full hands on deck now. We don't have time to bring her back and we can't risk her going back by herself. She'll be safest if she stays with the group," James replied. Looking directly at me, he said, "Looks like you're getting to shadow us a few days early after all. Just stay behind us and watch."

I nodded silently and felt myself shaking in fear and anger. I was going into an apparently dangerous situation with absolutely no knowledge on how to protect myself or anyone else. Max put his arm around my shoulders to comfort me and I felt some of that fear slip away.

Turning to James, Max argued, "Really James, you can't be serious. She hasn't even been here a full day. I won't allow her to be put danger like this. She doesn't even know how to work her bracelet for crying out loud!"

"There is no other choice," James said, not appearing overly confident but sounding firm in his decision. "We need to leave *now*, and she's going to need the experience sooner or later."

"Then later!" Max yelled, face flushed with anger. "It's not safe for her without even the most basic training!"

"There will be plenty of us there to watch her back; she won't be alone and she won't be in danger in a group full of experienced Patroni." James stated calmly. He started out the door, and the others began to follow him. "I know this isn't the best of circumstances, but we're out of options." Before Max could start his rebuttal, James cut him off, "I'll put you in charge of her since I know you'll insist anyway. Just keep her near you and bring up the rear."

Max must have thought that was an acceptable answer because he nodded firmly and took my hand. I was still nervous, but I was glad that Max was with me. No matter how dangerous things got, I knew he wouldn't let anything happen. I could see the emotion in his eyes when he spoke to James and wondered if he had feelings for me or was nervous just because I was new. I hoped it was the former. He gave my hand a small squeeze, and we headed off to join the others.

Sarah M. Ross

Four

We ran past the Commons to an area I'd never been before. It resembled like a park with a large grassy clearing in the center, the sort of place where under normal circumstances people would be playing soccer or having a picnic. At the edges of the open grassy area were benches and tables with a few people playing chess. Beyond the tables, some trees and a few buildings were visible. There were several elderly people and a few younger ones milling about. None of them seemed concerned. I realized these must be the spirits we guarded. They didn't appear frightened, so I figure they didn't know about the breech. All five of us ran past them and they seemed to ignore us for the most part. I tried to ask Max questions, but he kept a hold of my hand and we continued running towards the other side of the park. My legs were stronger today and I was glad I'd healed quite a bit in the five hours I slept. I gripped Max's hand tighter as we neared a small group of people and came to a stop. I recognized them from the Commons last night. Max kept us in the back of the pack, but I peered around him to see what was going on. This was difficult since he was a good five inches taller than me and much broader. There were way too many people to make out what was happening.

"What's happening? Where are we?" I whispered, still trying to see what in the world was going on. I've always been someone to face a challenge head on and not back down until I succeeded. I didn't like the idea of being held back and not helping if I could.

"There was a breech. A vampire got into to our realm and snatched two spirits before being spotted. This is where the vamp got through." Max said. He pointed at what looked like a small shed where you might keep supplies. There was a large blue door with hinges had most likely been torn off.

"Is that where the spirits come from?" I asked Max, still whispering.

"Yes, it's the entrance to the portal between the Earth realm and our realm. When spirits leaves their human bodies, they come through that door and wait here until their verdict. This time, a vampire clung to a spirit as it passed and entered. He stole that spirit and another one before someone noticed. The vampire wasn't smart enough to just to leave through the portal door again. Instead he got greedy. He's hiding out so he can take a few more."

"But all those spirits we just passed were just hanging out. Why aren't they running to safety?"

"We don't want to induce a mass panic; that would be worse. They probably just think it's a drill." Max replied. "James and another division leader are giving out orders. Some will stay and reinforce the door. Some will go hunting for the vamp. We'll probably stay with the spirits in this area and make sure no one else is taken."

The area seemed safe enough for the time being, but Max never let go of my hand and kept me close to him. I was more than happy to comply and took another step closer to him.

He smiled down at me and said, "Your bracelet has many of the tools that you'll need to do this job." I gawked at it, and I had no idea where it came from. It was just there. He let go of my hand for a minute to point out some features of the bracelet. "This is how we protect and defend. Think of it like a shield and sword all in one."

"But I have no idea how it works. I can see some symbols and stuff through my eyes, but I don't know how to make it function. Where's the keyboard?"

"You don't need one. Remember when James told you that you have more brain power now. That's all you need. Simply use your mind to command it, and the bracelet will comply. Let me give you an easy one. Think of a tent." He took my finger and pushed the bracelet as I pictured a tent. Immediately, I could see a camping tent in front of me.

"The tent is an invisible barrier that will hide you if you're in danger. Anything that threatens you won't be able to see inside of it. You can keep spirits inside of it, and they'll be invisible to anything that hasn't spotted them yet." A wide smile grew on my face as I began to understand how it worked.

"Okay, now think of a trumpet," Max said.

I cocked my head skeptically. "Why a trumpet?"

"It's easiest to think of object that you're already familiar with. A trumpet emits a sound at a wavelength werewolves can't tolerate. If you come into contact with one, just think of it and blow into it, and they'll be stunned for a moment and unable to move. This will allow you to get away before they can attack. But be careful, it only lasts for a minute or two. You'll need to run if you encounter one."

I nodded, "All right, I'm getting the hang of it. Show me another."

"Squirt gun," he said and I laughed.

"You've got to be kidding?"

"Nope, and this is a good one. Just try it." I thought of a squirt gun, ridiculous as it sounded, and one appeared in my hand. A stream of silvery liquid came spraying out of it when I pulled the trigger.

"Liquid silver, in a large dose, will kill a vampire." Max explained, "A small dose like this will disable a vampire enough for you to get away." I pulled the trigger again to test my aim and hit my target, the back of a nearby bench. I thought about these weapons and had an unwelcome realization.

"That's it?" I asked, astonished. "Just defensive weapons that allow me to run away? Nothing offensive to actually help or make a difference?" I thought my new position as a Patronus was going to make me a superhero, but it seemed like everything just helped me run away like a scared child, which was not who I was. I stood up for what I believed in or for someone who needed protecting. When I was a senior in high school I helped break up a fight. A gawky freshman girl was getting bullied by the "Mean Girls" clique. I had a black eye for two weeks that I wore proudly to let everyone know I wouldn't tolerate people picking on someone just because they were different. There was no way I was going to cower in a corner now when it really mattered.

"No, there are offensive weapons too, but you're still too new for those and haven't had any training. They'll come when you have more experience."

That made me feel a bit better, but I was still annoyed that I couldn't be more useful. I wanted to help right now. He suddenly bent down so we were almost eye to eye and close enough to kiss. I licked my lips and felt my pulse race at the thought.

"These are just the basics. I just want you safe today. I can't and I won't let anything happen to you." He pulled me into a strong hug and I could feel my body melting into him. We might be in the middle of danger or hell even a war, but with him embracing me like this, I couldn't think about anything but him. The embrace only lasted a few seconds and he let go and began talking to me again. "We need to get these spirits out of danger. First, it's imperative to move the spirits out of here and into a safe spot until we're sure the breech has been closed and no one else has snuck in." I peered at the vast, open field as Max spoke. There must be 30 elderly spirits in an area the size of a football field. And of course, they were all spread out. Some were trying to run to safety now that they realized there was a problem.

"And how exactly are we supposed to do that?" No way would we get all of these people gathered up. Max and I were the only people available and I had no idea what the hell I was doing.

"We have a safe house where they can go for now. Our bracelets are the only way to unlock it and open the door. Just tell people to go with you and take them there." He pointed to a building down a little hill to my right. It looked like a single wide trailer, and I didn't know exactly how safe that was supposed to be, but at this point what choice did I have?

"The vampire has been spotted deep in the woods, so we should be safe here for now. But I still don't feel comfortable leaving you to do this alone."

"Max, it's a field. I won't be out of your line of sight the whole time. And we can't get all of them if we stick together. We have to split up or risk losing spirits who have zero ability to protect themselves. It's not like I'm completely incompetent and can't put a few people in a house."

Max didn't like it, but as he glanced to his right and left, he saw his chances of getting everyone together at once diminishing rapidly. He had to trust me. We split up and Max took off to get the spirits farthest away from us and I started with the three people closest to me, making sure to stay in the open. They all appeared to be about 85 or 90 and just stood still, chatting amongst themselves. They were wearing nametags, which was very helpful. I began with an elderly gentleman, Mr. McFarland.

"Hello, I'm Lucy. Sorry to hear you died. I need you to come with me right now." I smiled, using my sweetest voice and tried to usher them with me, but they just ignored me and didn't move then turned back to their conversation. "Seriously, you need to come right now!" I said in a more firm tone. What was with these people, did they *want* to become vampires? *Twilight* was awesome and all, but I can't see Mr. McFarland becoming the next Edward. "Let's move people!" I put my hands on their backs to guide them forward only to have Mr. McFarland poke me in my knee with his cane.

"Ow!" I exclaimed, rubbing my knee disbelievingly. "I can't believe you poked me!"

"Listen here, Missy! I've waited seventeen years to be reunited with my Eloisa and I'm not leaving here until I find her." The two matronly ladies with him both nodded silently.

Mrs. Goldberg nodded her head so vigorously her ginger wig was knocked off kilter, and little gray hairs poked out from underneath. "Me too! I promised my Albert I would wait for him. I didn't break a promise in our 52 years of marriage and I won't break it now." She then crossed her hands over her chest and "hmphed" at me.

I just shook my head! I couldn't believe these old farts were giving me attitude. Here I was trying to help them and they wanted to give me lip! Enough was enough, so grabbed the most petite person there, Mrs. Kremnik according to her nametag, and picked her up in a fireman's hold. She was extremely startled by my actions and immediately began screaming (as if that wouldn't draw any unwanted attention to us!). I started heading down the little hill intending to secure her in the safe house at the bottom and realized I needed to walk faster because the others were smacking me in the ass with their canes. This job was going to be a lot harder than I had originally thought. I made it down the small hill and to the safe house. I saw the security pad and on a hunch, held my bracelet up to it. There was a small beep and I could hear the locks release.

"Just stay here, Mrs. Kremnik. I'll be back for you as soon as I can." I plopped her down and ran back up the hill to grab another one. As soon as I got to the top of the hill, I glanced behind me only to see a little grey head pop out of the door to the safe house and scoot outside. Crap! Apparently I didn't make sure the door was locked again before I left–rookie mistake! It was like herding cats. Once you get one where you want it, three more have escaped and run off to do their own thing.

"This job will be the death of me," I muttered to myself, shaking my head at my own absurdity (Hello! I was dead already!). I grabbed the remaining two by the hand and began pulling them down the hill amid cries of "help" and "get off me". I ignored them for the most part and continued down the hill. I opened the door with my bracelet and shoved them inside. "Stay put!" I commanded and made sure the lock was secure this time.

I peered up the hill to try to see where Mrs. Kremnik had disappeared to and spotted Max carrying another elderly lady gently in his arms towards me. As he came closer, the bright shining sunlight in the meadow highlighted his thick black hair now tousled from running. His smile made me melt, and I felt immediate relief from the stress of the situation. He set the woman down, careful to keep a hold of her until he was sure that she was steady on her feet. She thanked him and gave him a kiss on the cheek before he unlocked the door with his bracelet, and she stepped inside and closed the door without a fight. With a small beep, the locks went back on.

"How did you do that? I couldn't even get them to stop poking me with their canes!" I teased him.

He winked at me and bent down to whisper in my ear, "It's my magical charm."

I thought about that for a second and decided that's exactly what it was. If I'd gotten to be carried by him, his firm chest muscles rippling beneath me and feeling his broad arms safely around me, I'd want to bend down and give him a kiss. Or two. Or ten.

"Did you get everyone inside?" he asked, scanning the area.

"No, I had an escapee. These people do not like me at all and had no desire to stay put." I replied, exasperation apparent in my voice. Max placed his arm around me to comfort me, and its effect was immediate.

"It's only your first day. It gets better, I promise. Hell, my first day I had a lady bite me right here!" he said, pointing to his chest. "I had to double check to make sure she wasn't a vampire in disguise."

More lustful thoughts swirled in my head, but I shook them out, quickly realizing this was not the time or place. I tried to focus on our current problem rather than my growing desire for Max.

Max continued, "We need to find her before the vamp does. Stay here and lock yourself in the safe house with the others. I'm going to go find her. I'll be back in a moment." I knew he was right, but I didn't have to like it. Max took off towards the west, and I opened the door and started inside the safe house. Just then, out of the corner of my eye I spotted Mrs. Kremnik. She was next to a group of what resembled cabins and had her back to me. I knew Max would never see her, and I hesitated for a moment before decided to run and get her real quick. It would just take a minute and I didn't see any harm in going.

As I proceeded back up the hill, I glanced around and saw that no one else was in the area any more, giving it an eerie feel. I made it to the top of the hill and turned right towards a few other deserted looking buildings where a person could hide. I reached the door of the first building I saw. It reminded me of a rustic cabin that you'd find near a lake and I thought it was a perfect place for her to hide. I opened the door and poked my head inside.

"Mrs. Kremnik? Are you in here?" I called out. The building was so dark I couldn't see a thing. I stopped to think for a moment and wondered what else my bracelet could do. "Flashlight" I said out loud as I thought of one. Immediately there was a glow coming from my arm. "Sweet! I love this thing!" I aimed the flashlight away from me and began to scan the room. It looked empty, but just as I was ready to turn it off and move on to the next building, I noticed a lump in the far right corner big enough to be a person.

"Mrs. Kremnik? Is that you?" I coaxed sweetly. "You really need to come with me. I promise I'll help you find your loved ones later." I approached the lump cautiously and realized it was just a sack of soccer balls with a tarp over them. "Get a grip, Luc" I muttered to myself. I couldn't believe a few harmless soccer balls were putting my nerves on edge. Well, them and the dark room. I turned and reached for the door in order to leave and check the next building.

Just as my hand touched the doorknob, I felt an ice-cold breath on the back of my neck that made all my hairs stand on end. I was in trouble. Nothing that cold would come from a living being. I mustered the courage to face whatever it was. I whipped myself around only to come face to face with a giant pair of red eyes, the kind in nightmares. I caught a brief glimpse of fangs before I dropped my conjured up flashlight, and it disappeared back into my bracelet. The whole room plummeted into darkness, save for those red eyes moving toward me.

Sarah M. Ross

Five

"Screaming won't do you any good," snarled the voice behind those eyes. It was the worst voice I'd ever heard, and it made me shudder all over. The voice sounded like it belonged to a chain smoking, whiskey drinking alcoholic with a ten pack a day habit and a bad case of laryngitis. Sharp nails raking down a chalkboard would have sounded more pleasant. As much as I wanted to freak out, I knew that would only hurt and not help. I forced myself to stay still for a moment and tried to stop shaking, knowing it would betray my fear.

"Do you hear me screaming?" I spat back, mustering any courage I had left. I would not give him the satisfaction of knowing he scared the pants off of me.

"Feisty! I like it." He dragged a sharp pointed fingernail across my shoulder and down my arm. I felt the skin break slightly and tiny drops of blood pebble to the surface. It took everything inside me to keep from flinching. "I can hear your heart racing. I know you're afraid," he continued. "I only wanted one of the old ones, but I'll be a hero when I bring you back with me."

His body pushed up against mine and he was excited. That feeling alone was enough to cause vomit to rise in my mouth and my stomach contents to curdle. I tried to swallow it back down. He ground himself against me with a smile that told me it was just the beginning and he intended to enjoy himself. I couldn't control the tears as they fell down my face. At least I wouldn't scream, I refused to give him the satisfaction. I had to try to regain some semblance of control of the situation. I couldn't let myself and my team down on my first day.

"I'm not going anywhere with you, freak!" I half screamed, getting less afraid than angry at the situation I'd stupidly put myself in. I refused to be a victim. I would not let him win. My mind raced thinking of everything that James had told me earlier, but it was all history and nothing that I could apply now. I refused to give up. There *had* to be something James had said that I could use, I just needed to remember. I thought about all of the vampire movies and books I'd read in the past and the ways to kill them. Sunlight, stakes, garlic, and mirrors were all that would come to mind, but would they work? Complicating things, the crazy eyed, gruff voiced vampire was now holding my arm firmly against him so I couldn't get to my bracelet to try any of those things. I thought back to what I'd seen in the room earlier while I still had the flashlight, but all I could recall were the tarp and those soccer balls, and I didn't think the vampire was up for a scrimmage. I was thinking fast as I tried to wiggle my arm free, but he just tightened his grip.

"All your wiggling is getting me more excited. I love foreplay." He boasted with a sneer that made me gag. No way to hold the vomit back now. I spat at him and tried to stomp on his foot but missed because he moved slightly in order to wipe his face. I needed to do something quick, but what? The best thing I could come up with was the classic wooden stake. Hey, it was classic for a reason, right? I imagined with all my might and felt it slide into my hand. Granted, it was the hand I couldn't move but hey, it was progress.

"Now, come quietly and I won't hurt you too much," the Nosferatu wannabe barked at me. He tried to push me towards the door but I planted my feet and refused to move, knowing my odds of survival worsened if he was able to move me to another location. Apparently that was the wrong move because he backhanded me so hard I saw stars and fell to my knees. I could taste blood in my mouth and knew I'd have a giant bruise on my cheek. Maybe even a fractured cheekbone. I resisted the urge to spit out the blood because it would just add fuel to the vampire's fire. I swallowed it, swiping my tongue around my mouth to clean it. I scurried to my feet and tried to run away from him. I just needed to put some distance between us so I had a chance at surviving this. It was still pitch black, and I hoped that meant he couldn't see me either. I purposefully moved in a zigzag pattern just in case and placed my body flat against a pillar in the middle of the room. His voice was getting louder, so I knew he was getting closer. I didn't know which direction he would attack me from next. I began to take quiet, baby steps backwards, trying to be as gradual as possible. If I could just get to the door…

In one smooth motion he grabbed me by my hair and yanked me back to him. A searing pain exploded on the back of my head and I choked out a cry. He kept hold of my hair with one hand and grabbed my arm with the other. It felt like he was pulling my hair out by the roots and I could feel blood trickling down my neck. I began to panic that it would be enough to send him over the edge, but he still didn't try to bite me.

"You will do as I command!" he bellowed at me. He sneered and tried to move me again. Apparently this wasn't good foreplay for him anymore. I was proud of that small victory.

"Like I already said, asshat, I'm not going anywhere with you." I stomped on his toe with my heel using every ounce of strength I had. It was just enough for him to loosen the grip on my hand, and I swung the stake at his chest. I miraculously got the tip of it embedded into his chest, but I didn't have the strength to break the chest bone. He just looked down at it and began laughing. My eyes got wide with the realization that not only did I not do any damage, I'd made him angrier. He grabbed my hand again before I could do anything else and he used his free hand to remove the stake. He tossed it away and continued laughing.

"Wow, you really must be new you foolish, foolish child." The anger in his eyes was clearly visible, and I braced to be hit again, but nothing came. Instead, he pushed me down to the ground, and I landed hard on my butt. He knelt next to me. "Have they taught you nothing? Wooden stakes are useless to us. Myth! But now you've reached my last nerve and I think I need a drink to calm me down." He grabbed my hair tighter and pulled me towards him. I felt the pain screaming from my scalp and it took everything I had not to pass out. I felt his cold, putrid breath against my skin and something sharp pressing down against my throat and had a moment of sheer panic. I was going to die for the second time.

"NO!" I screamed as loud as I could. It startled him and I wrenched my arm free. I suddenly remembered what Max told me and manically started mumbling "Squirt gun, squirt gun, squirt gun" putting everything I had into it. I felt it in my hand and cocked it, aiming for the vampire. He was just regaining his composure and his fangs were closing in on my neck. I aimed for the inside of his mouth and squeezed the trigger like a kid at a carnival filling up a balloon.

The silvery liquid shot out and landed directly in its target. Smoke began to pour out from inside of his mouth and fury overtook him. He couldn't scream because his mouth was disintegrating, but he didn't need to speak for me to know any ounce of mercy he might have shown me had just gone out the window. I didn't waste any time as I scrambled towards the door and reached for the handle. Just as I grasped it, the vampire caught my arm with both of his hands and twisted, giving me the hardest Indian burn I've ever had. I felt the bones breaking and fell to the ground in agony. He kicked my stomach, and I threw up. He continued kicking me as I rolled onto my side and curled up into a ball to try to protect myself.

It was the last thing I could do. I hoped he'd let me die quickly, but after burning his mouth like that, I knew it was unlikely. He slashed at my back with claws, and it felt like a cat of nine tails gouging holes in my skin. He continued to punch and kick, pummeling me. I felt myself passing out and knew there was nothing else I could do. He stopped his assault and stared down at me.

"You had your fun," he began, the words no longer fully formed. Pieces of his decomposing mouth fell on me as he spoke, "Now I'll have mine." He methodically came towards me and bent down. I could feel his fangs scraping against my skin as he crawled on top of me starting at my feet. I felt his hands on my body and several times felt myself being stabbed by his fangs on my calves, thighs, stomach, and chest. I began to shake involuntarily. I stared at his now distorted face and he smiled a horrific smile before biting down on my neck. I had lost and I knew it. I thought of Max smiling at me. I wanted to have one nice thought in my mind before I died. Again.

Sarah M. Ross

Six

Consciousness slowly came back to me. I didn't know how long I had lain there bleeding. I didn't know how much blood I'd lost. To my horror, the vampire was still on top of me, grinding against me and languorously licking small trickles of blood from my bare torso. I tried not to think about it. I didn't want to know what horrible things had been done to me. I was too weak to move. I knew there was no hope for me. I wished for death. I closed my eyes again hoping it would come quickly and slipped back into unconsciousness.

The time drifted imperceptibly and I was in and out of consciousness. I opened my eyes. The room started spinning and my thoughts were jumbled. I squeezed my eyes shut, trying to remember why I felt like death warmed over. Just as I began to feel myself slipping back into the darkness, the doors of the room burst open allowing light to stream in and overtake the darkness that enveloped me. A red haze blurred my vision, and I tried to blink it away but failed. My eyes burned, but I kept blinking to clear the blood away. I could see the silhouettes of two people standing in the doorway. My vision was too blurred to know who they were, but I hoped it was someone who could help me. Through the haze, I could discern that they had kicked in the door and were looking around frantically. I was half hidden behind the pillar and was too weak to call for help. I turned my face towards the light and the figures standing in the doorway, praying with all my might that they would see me.

As the larger one's face turned in my direction, it stopped. Whoever it was had spotted me. Relief washed over me, but it was short lived. I heard an angry, desperate scream.

"No!" wailed a deep voice, which I immediately knew belonged to Max. I could hear the pain in his voice and wondered if I was dead yet again. Was he seeing my dead body? The second voice muttered multiple curses and rushed inside, scanning the room for threats. I was pretty sure based on the Southern drawl the second voice was Adam, but maybe I was only hoping. I closed my eyes and drifted away again.

"I got him," the Southern voice announced victoriously, bringing me back to reality once more. I blinked repeatedly, desperate to clear my vision so I could see his face. Max was already rushing towards me, and he slid to his knees, my blood coated his jeans. He very gently placed my head in his lap and began stroking my hair. I thought he was doing it just to sooth me, but then I realized he was clearing the hair away from my wounds. My hair was sticky with blood, and Max was trying not to hurt me as he cleared it to inspect my neck. The lights had turned on, and it was easier to see his face. I tried unsuccessfully to reach my hand up to touch him, and I couldn't make my mouth form words, so I just stared at his eyes hoping he'd find my questions in them. His eyes were wide as he saw the damage, and I wondered just how bad it was. I dug deep and found the strength, opening my mouth to ask but felt his finger gently on my lips.

"Shh, don't try to talk. The vampire tore at your throat pretty badly, and I need you to stay as still as you can until help comes. There are some other wounds too and..." He choked off a sob and I knew it must be pretty bad. "But you'll be fine. I've already called for help, so it shouldn't be much longer." His voice tried to sound confident and sure, but his eyes betrayed him. He didn't turn his gaze to see if anyone was coming, he just kept stroking my hair and studying me as tears welled in his eyes. He had torn off his shirt to use it to apply pressure to the wound at my throat. The pain was incomprehensible, but with Max there it was more tolerable.

"Don't worry, you'll be fine. I promise I won't let anything else happen to you. It was my fault, I should have never let you go off by yourself." I opened my mouth to argue that it was in fact my own stupidity that caused this, but I remembered he told me not talk. I simply shook my head very slowly, just once, to object.

With the lights on I could see that the other person in the room was indeed Adam. He had a long silver sword in his hand that was covered in blood and a metal medical syringe in the other. He was pacing the room and looked nervous. I couldn't see the vampire anywhere, but the blood on the sword made me hopeful.

As if speaking my thoughts, Max turned to Adam and asked, "Is it taken care of?"

Adam nodded but kept pacing.

"So why are you still pacing? Go see if help is coming!" Max commanded, clearly needing to do something while feeling so helpless.

Adam stopped for a moment and focused at both of us and spoke in a low voice. "I caught the vamp, and he's been taken care of." That was the best news I'd heard all day. I breathed a sigh of relief– metaphorically speaking because my throat was still too torn to take an actual deep breath. I didn't feel bad that he was dead. I'm not one who took pity on criminals, I believed very strongly in Karma. He tried to hurt and capture others, and he hurt me– badly. I just hoped it wasn't too bad or too late. "But," Adam continued, "I don't think he was alone. When I cornered him, he was muttering for help as I drew my sword and took out the syringe. Why would he do that if he sneaked through the portal by himself?

I have this feeling, this wasn't an isolated attack." With that, any relief I felt vanished.

Just then, the door opened and several official looking people with medical equipment came in. I still couldn't move, but I tried. I knew it was looking bad for me, but I was honestly too afraid to hear the verdict. I was brave when it came to helping my family or friends, but seeing my own blood made me lightheaded and dizzy. I squeezed my eyes shut and kept them that way. I felt Max move, and my head was no longer resting in his lap. His hands also moved from my neck and hair, but not away from me completely. He gently slid his hand down my arm and took my hand in his. Even though they asked him to back off so they could do their jobs, he wouldn't leave me. That thought filled me with joy, and I willed my body not to give up. If Max wasn't giving up on me, I couldn't give up on myself.

My eyes were still shut, but I could feel several sets of hands on me. I was lifted and placed on a stretcher, but we didn't leave the building quite yet. A liquid was poured onto my neck. It startled me at first as I thought it was more of my blood leaking out, but then it started to burn. My eyes shot open as my neck felt like it had caught fire. The woman in front of me was holding a bottle, and she continued pouring its contents onto me. I screamed so loudly it startled her, and I squeezed Max's hand so hard, I'm sure I must have broken something. The woman, after regaining her composure, watched me closely and explained, "I know it hurts, but it's cauterizing your wounds. We need to stop the bleeding as fast as possible, and you need to stop screaming so you don't cause more damage."

I stopped screaming, but didn't lessen the grip on Max's hand. He didn't seem to mind and just smiled at me. The pain was more intense than the bites had been and I ground my teeth to keep from crying out in agony. The woman finally finished pouring the liquid over my neck and gave the order to move me. As they rushed me out the door, my hand slipped from Max's. I tried grabbing for it again, but he was too far behind me now. He yelled for me and told me that he was coming with me and to just hang on. I was loaded into an ambulance and rushed back to the room where I'd first woken up. As they transferred me to the bed I glanced around for a familiar face, but found none. There were about ten people in the room, all poking and prodding me. I had no idea what they were doing, but I knew instantly when the pain meds were administered. My eyes slid shut unwillingly and I felt so much better–I felt nothing at all.

I became aware of monitors beeping. I opened my eyes and looked around. Max and Cassie were next to me. James and Adam were leaning against the back wall. When they noticed I was awake, they took a step forward.

"Lucy? You gave us a real scare there, sweetie. How are you feeling?" Cassie asked in her most soothing tone. "Is there anything we can get you? More pain meds?" She nodded at Adam who nodded at her and left the room, presumably to get a doctor. I tried to speak, but my throat felt like someone had taken a sandblaster to it.

"You're not going to be able to speak normally for a little while yet." Max informed me. "Between the damage to your neck and the cauterizing agent, your throat's been through the wringer."

I nodded and made a W with my fingers, holding it to my chin. I hoped someone else knew sign language.

James must have, because he responded to the group, "She wants some water." Max turned to get it and I smiled in appreciation at James. He signed back, "You're welcome," and leaned back against the wall. I struggled to sit up in the bed and Max helped prop me. I stared at James and signed, "Am I okay?"

"What's she saying?" Cassie asked, clearly confused by our silent conversation.

"She's just asking if she's okay. You are Lucy. You're going to be fine," James explained.

I sighed and put my head back against the pillow. Adam entered with a nurse who pushed a syringe full of something into my IV. My eyes became heavy and I took Max's hand in mine before drifting off again.

When I woke up again, everyone was in the room with me, but time had obviously passed. They'd changed clothes. Cassie and Adam were playing cards in the corner, James was eating food from a Chinese takeout carton, and Max was sleeping in the chair next to my bed–still holding my hand. A broad smile swept across my face as I watched him sleep for a moment and my stomach fluttered when I saw our fingers entwined.

I decided to try out my voice, praying that my throat had healed enough to speak. "Hey, guys." I started, surprised by the hoarseness of my voice, but happy I could speak at all. "Come here often?"

Everyone stopped what they were doing and stared at me. Max bolted upright and began checking the monitors, apparently making sure my numbers and levels were okay. My poor attempt at a joke seemed to break the tension and get a laugh out of everyone except Max. He still looked really worried. Cassie seemed to pick up on this, and she tried to lighten the mood a little further.

"Couldn't get enough of this place, Luc? Had to rekindle the relationship your ass had with that bed?"

I smiled at her and tried to sit up.

Max stood up but didn't help right away. "You sure you're okay enough to move?" he asked, using the back of his hand to check the temperature of my forehead.

"Enough to sit up," I responded honestly. He must have been satisfied with his scan of my monitors because he helped me into a sitting position. "Thanks," I said sheepishly. I felt a little better now that I wasn't lying flat on my back and was able to take a deep breath for the first time. The look on his face revealed he was upset, but I wasn't sure why. I was feeling much better, and I wasn't dead. These were both signs of good news in my book. "So how long was I out this time?" I asked. I peered down was relieved to see that I didn't have the giant cuffs on again, and I wasn't half naked like last time.

"Six days total," James replied. "You were lucky. The vamp must have thought no one would find you because he was taking his time draining you. He didn't want to turn you, he was just aiming to kill and he was going to do it slowly to make you suffer," he said it so matter-of-factly I winced at the words.

Max shot him a look that I'm sure had R rated words behind it and then turned his gaze back towards me. "That's not what's important," he whispered as he rubbed circles over my palm with his thumb. "He didn't succeed, and now he's the one who's dead, though I wish his death could have been more painful than it was."

"Yeah, next time I'll try to kill him slower for you, man." Adam retorted, obviously offended by Max's remarks. "Or maybe I'll just leave him to you since you think you could have done better."

Max sighed. "You know that's not what I meant. I am eternally grateful for what you did. I just wish he would have had to suffer more. And I wish we'd stop having this same argument. You would have felt the same way if it was Cassie and you know it."

At that, Adam moved closer to Cassie and reached for her hand. "You're right, I know that. I'm just as frustrated as you are with what happened to Lucy. I don't like to see any of our own get hurt."

"I can't thank you guys enough for what you did. I owe you two everything," I said with all sincerity. "But really, I'm feeling much better." The pain in my throat was gone and I only had a little soreness in the areas that took the worst blows: my check where he struck me, my arm where it snapped, and my back where he kicked me repeatedly. I knew those injuries were healing fast by how quickly I was recovering and was optimistic I would be back to myself in no time. "When can I go back to the Dwelling? As much as I enjoy hanging out in this place, I want to go home."

"That shouldn't be too much of a problem. The worst of your injuries have healed and you don't need the constant monitoring anymore," James remarked. "Just let me go clear it with a few people." He turned and walked out of the room. Cassie stood up from her card game and led Adam to the back of the room. I could see her whispering to him, and they looked lost in their own world. That left me sort of alone with Max. He still wasn't smiling and the worry lines on his face were more predominant now.

"I promise, I'm feeling much better," I told him, hoping to assuage his worries. "I can't thank you enough. If you guys didn't find me when you did, I don't even want to think about how much worse it could have been. I can't believe I was stupid enough to go in there alone. Patronus or not–I know better than to go into a dark and spooky place alone when there's a bad guy on the loose."

"No, it's completely my fault," he responded, his eyes becoming misty. "I didn't take the threat seriously enough. I should have kept you with me. I never should have let you leave my sight. I'm so sorry, Lucy, can you ever forgive me?" He looked so hurt, like his entire world had just come crashing down.

"There's nothing to forgive. I'm the one who should be asking forgiveness. You told me to stay where I was. You knew the dangers, and I apparently didn't take them seriously enough. I should have listened instead of trying to fix everything on my own. I just thought it was best to find everyone and keep them safe. I didn't think we could do that if I'd been stuck waiting for you. I hated the idea of not helping and just sitting around when people needed me. It was all my stupid fault. Please don't blame yourself." I pleaded.

He didn't say anything else, just sat on the edge of the bed watching at me. It was nice; it felt like he was trying to memorize every detail on my face so when he closed his eyes he could still picture me.

I hated to interrupt his gazing, but I had so many questions now that I wasn't so worried about dying. I'm sure I was still in a state of shock based on how I was taking all of this in stride, but I needed some answers. I started with the most basic, "How bad was it?"

I could tell Max didn't want to answer. It hurt him to recall the details, but I had to know. "You're safe now, that's what's important."

Remembering the vampire grinding against me caused more bile to rise in my throat. "Max, please tell me. I need to know. I think by not knowing, I'll imagine the very worst scenario possible. I'll feel that every horrific thing that could have been done to a person was done to me. I need to know that's not true. I need to know what was done, so I can stop imagining the possibilities. That hurts more than reality." My façade of being okay was cracking along with my voice, but I pressed on. He needed to understand that I wasn't asking out of curiosity. I needed to know so I could face it and move on. It's always the wondering and what ifs that drove me crazy. I couldn't go there. When my baby sister Jessica was diagnosed with cancer, I went and researched everything I could on the topic. I needed to know as much about the disease as possible so I could be prepared. I needed to know so I could form a plan. Ignorance was my worst nightmare when dealing with tragedy.

Max took a deep breath and slowly exhaled. I knew he was accepting that I needed to know, but it was going to kill him to tell me. And he'd tell me anyway. "He bit you so ferociously that if you were still human, you'd look like a burn victim with the amount of scarring you'd have," he started. "He drank from you. Almost three pints of blood in total were lost. One more and you might not have made it. He broke your arm and three ribs. Your cheekbone was caved in and required extensive reconstruction. You had deep lacerations down your back where he clawed at you. Your spleen was ruptured and your kidneys were bruised." He stopped for a second. I knew that had been the easy part, and I braced myself for his next words. "Your clothes were ripped to shreds by his claws, leaving you exposed for him to bite wherever he pleased. There was blood smeared on your body, apparently because he was rubbing blood all over you and then licking it off. He was torturing you leisurely. You must have really pissed him off."

"Yeah well, I guess I didn't have the most pleasant disposition when I made his acquaintance," I teased shakily, trying to use humor to ease some of my fears. It wasn't working and I couldn't hold on to this brave act much longer as I came face to face with the reality of the situation. Tears welled in my eyes and I tried to take a deep breath, but all I could think about was him touching my body and violating me in the worst possible way. "Did he…" I couldn't make the words finish coming out of my mouth. I wanted the answer, but couldn't ask the question.

Max couldn't make the words come out either. He just gazed deep into my eyes and shook his head from side to side slowly. Overwhelmed with relief, I burst out crying. I sobbed and sobbed not able to control myself any longer. Max put his arms around me and held me tight, crying as well. He held me so tight it hurt the bruises that covered my body, but I didn't want him to ever let me go.

Through my tears I could hear him murmuring to himself, "Never again, never going to lose you again," and I cried even harder. Cassie and Adam heard our crying and came over to see what was wrong. Neither spoke, but Cassie came from the other side and hugged me tight too. Adam joined in and we had a long, awkward group hug while I bawled my eyes out. Never in my life had I been so afraid of a question. And never in my life had I been so relieved to hear an answer that wasn't spoken.

Sarah M. Ross

Seven

After a few hours and another round of tests to be sure all of my internal injuries had completely healed, James worked his magic and got me released so I could go back to my own bed to sleep. I was left with a bunch of bruises and soreness from head to toe and those would heal with rest. The idea of sleeping surrounded by the things that gave me the most comfort sounded heavenly. I wanted nothing more than to curl up in bed wrapped in my favorite blanket and pretend the last few days hadn't happened. I was completely cool with living in denial a little while longer. The idea of being alone again, however, made me cringe. Even though I knew the danger had passed, I wasn't ready to face the world alone. I insisted everyone come back to our Dwelling to hang out and refused to take no for an answer. I needed normalcy to take my mind off of what could have happened

Even though I was well enough to walk, Max refused to let me. I begrudgingly accepted the wheelchair ride back to my Dwelling to keep from hearing his complaining and set off with everyone in tow. I winced slightly as we hit a few bumps on the trip back to my room. I asked James why I still had pain even though my injuries were healed. He explained it was allowed purposefully so we remained grounded and didn't get an invincibility complex. Apparently, there had been a time when no injury could cause pain to a Patronus. It made some act foolishly and irresponsibly, causing several spirits to suffer as a result. Now, even though death is rare due to our enhanced healing powers, it's the pain that reminds us to take precautions.

    We arrived and I let Max help me into bed. It wasn't much of a hardship. It didn't matter that there were three other people with us. I ignored them all and continued to stare openly at Max. Now that I wasn't in danger and was still a little high on pain meds, I couldn't get enough of him. I was like a moth to a flame, drawn to him inexplicably and unable to keep away. If I learned anything from the experience, it was to take life by the horns before it was too late. He saved my life, and I wanted to show just how much I appreciated it. I wanted to be near him, knowing that I would feel safer if I was touching him, even just holding his hand. I was connected to him. I felt a sense of contentment when he was with me that I couldn't explain. It felt like being away at college for months and months, and then finally coming home for Christmas–that peaceful feeling like you were meant to be there and nothing could go wrong. Cassie was half smiling at me out of the corner of her mouth and Adam was looking at me strangely. I forced myself to turn my attention away before I made a complete ass of myself and suggested we watch a movie. I needed to lose myself in the Hollywood world of make believe for a few more hours; something to take my mind off of the horror of the last few days and the urgings my body seemed to have every time Max entered my line of sight. Everyone settled in around my room. Adam took the floor with Cassie and James took the only chair I had, which left Max with nowhere to go other than to sit with me on the bed.

    Cassie rushed into the kitchen to play hostess and get drinks and popcorn, but not before giving me a wink that made me squirm, knowing she knew what I was thinking. I was glad Max chose to sit on the bed with me, even though he was sitting awkwardly on the opposite edge and feigning being comfortable. I contemplated telling him to come closer and sit next to me, but realized how uncomfortable it might make him feel. Yes, I wanted him next to me, holding me and keeping me safe. But we were co-workers and hardly knew each other. I sensed he wanted to be next to me too, but it was a little awkward to express those feelings with our entire team in the same room. I bit my lip nervously, trying to think of something to say.

At that moment, Cassie came back in with snacks for all and turned the lights out to start the movie. She had thankfully chosen a comedy to keep the mood light and I tried to get in to it. In the end, I didn't watch any of it. Instead, I thought about these people surrounding me who had taken me in and made me one of them. I surveyed the room and spotted Cassie and Adam cuddling and feeding each other popcorn, and James laughing at the antics of Adam Sandler. Finally I turned to Max, who winked as I spotted him. I winked back, put my head down on the pillow, and allowed myself to relax and drift off to sleep.

I opened my eyes and saw the movie had ended. The TV was just a blue screen and the sound was muted. Cassie and Adam were gone, most likely to her room, and James was nowhere to be seen either. Max was still there, sleeping in the chair that James had previously occupied. I could see it was still dark out and glanced at the time, 3:30 in the morning. I untangled myself from the blanket and tip-toed over to Max, placing it over him. I left the room and headed to the kitchen to get a drink. I saw James passed out on the couch and tried not to wake him as I grabbed a bottle of water from the fridge. I turned to go back to my room and ran directly into Max. I gasped, then quickly covered my mouth with my hand to keep the sound in. We'd all had a long couple of days, and I didn't want to wake anyone up.

"Oh my gravy, you startled me!" I whispered to him, taking several steps backwards while trying to slow my now racing heart. He didn't reply, just put a finger to his mouth signaling me to stay quiet. He took my hand and led me back to my room. Once inside, he closed the door.

"I'm sorry, Lucy, I didn't mean to scare you. I just got worried when I saw that you were gone," he replied softly. I held up the bottle of water for him to see. He nodded in understanding, and I went to sit back on the bed, opening the bottle and taking a long drink. He didn't come in any further, although I could see him eyeing the bed. Not getting my hopes up, I reasoned he probably wanted to make sure I rested more so I continued to heal. My assumption was confirmed when he announced, "I guess I should let you go back to sleep," and headed for the door. My chest tightened at the thought of him leaving and being alone for the first time since the attack.

"Stay," I begged softly, and he paused. "I don't think I can be alone yet. Will you stay?"

He didn't turn around, keeping his back to me with his hand on the door. I was sure he'd refuse, but still I held my breath awaiting his answer. He stayed that way for a minute before he nodded. "Yes, of course. I can stay."

I lay back, feeling relieved and excited all at once. "Thank you."

He walked back towards the bed and pulled the covers up over me before he went to sit in the chair. "Max," I blurted out, and he turned back towards me. I propped my arm up, resting my elbow on the pillow and just stared at him. Neither of us said anything aloud, but our eyes held the words we were both too nervous to speak. The chair was not where I wanted him, and it wasn't where he wanted to be. I needed him next to me. I needed to feel his arms around me. I yearned to know what that felt like. I knew with certainty my heart would explode if I didn't feel them around me within the next minute. To my relief, he stood and came back without hesitation. He scooped me up and held me tight. The ache from not touching him melted away and my heart and soul danced together in gratification. Being surrounded by his embrace brought me a euphoria that most people only got through chemical means. I closed my eyes and inhaled, making sure none of my senses were deprived of this amazing experience.

We stayed like that for a long time. Neither of us talking or moving, just enjoying the moment. Eventually, he repositioned me so he was half sitting up, his back was against the headboard. My body lay against his, and I snuggled in so I could hear his heartbeat and the evenness of his breathing. I listened to it for hours, the steady rhythm lulling any lingering anxiety from me.

With any previous cuddling, I'd never fit comfortably next to the guys I'd dated. I was always too tall and cuddling felt awkward. With Max, however, I fit like a glove. My lean muscular frame felt petite in his broad arms, and the sense of belonging in this place at this time fell naturally upon me. I wanted to stay wrapped up in him forever. I thought back to my favorite Shakespearian scene, when Romeo begs for the bird he hears to be the nightingale and not the lark. He knew the lark would signal the end of his wonderful first night with Juliet. I understood the words in class when we read it, but it wasn't until now that I understood the emotion behind it. I never was so happy to see the moon and hoped upon hope that I'd never hear the lark.

The sound of movement throughout the house roused me from my slumber and I opened my eyes. Max was still holding me, and I smiled not wanting to move for fear of waking him up and having this end. I tilted my head to gaze up at him, and to my surprise he smiled back at me. I wondered how long he'd been sitting there watching my sleep. Oh god, I hoped I didn't have eye crusties! I raised my hands to my eyes to check and exhaled a deep sigh of relief when I felt none.

"Hey, good morning," Max greeted me softly. "How are you feeling?"

"Amazing," I confessed dreamily. His voice alone made me melt like a chocolate bar left in the sun. "I've never slept better."

"I'm glad." His hands tracing the outline of my face as I stared up at him. "I don't know what I would have done if you would have died."

My eyes widened and hope swelled in my chest. "I wouldn't have survived without you," I said softly, refusing to tear my eyes away from his face. His blue eyes twinkled in the morning sun and there was no stopping the smile that formed on my face.

"You look so beautiful when you sleep," Max leaned in, whispering in my ear. "I couldn't keep my eyes off of you."

I blushed at his words, but couldn't form any of my own. His hand, which was tracing the outline of my face moved down my neck, and he leaned down towards me. My heart raced a million miles a minute in excitement and I placed my arms around his neck.

"Lucy," he whispered.

"Yes, Max?"

"I loved holding you in my arms last night. It felt so right–so natural. Like you were meant to be there."

"Two pieces of a puzzle," I sighed, leaning closer to kiss him, but he hesitated.

"It's late, the others are probably wondering where we are," he sighed, but paused before continuing. "I guess I should go…" Despite his words, he made no move to leave.

"Breakfast?" I suggested, anything to spend a little more time with him. I was disappointed he hadn't kissed me. It seemed like he wanted to, but for some reason he held back. Did he think it was too soon after my attack? Or maybe something simple like we had both just woken up and neither of us had brushed our teeth yet. Maybe my morning breath was really bad this morning…

"Sounds great." He tried stretching a little, but didn't get far with me practically on top of him. I sat up, unhappy to relinquish our time together so soon, but it was necessary. He stood up and searched for his shoes.

"Let me just brush my teeth and hair first," I said, running my fingers through my knotted hair.

"I probably should do the same. Can I meet you in the Commons, say fifteen minutes?"

I smiled happily. "It's a date."

I opened the bedroom door to see him out and was taken aback when Cassie and Adam were standing right outside of it. Adam looked down, guilt over eavesdropping written all over his face. Cassie just beamed at us. "Breakfast sounds great guys! We'll join you!"

"Oh...ah...um...of course," I stammered. I was hoping for more alone time with Max, but Cassie beamed happily. I just couldn't say no to her. "We'll just meet you there."

"Hey, thanks for inviting me Cass," I heard behind me. James was staggering down the hall rubbing sleep from his eyes and not wearing a shirt. I had never seen him like this before and didn't quite know what to make of it. He was undeniably handsome and drool worthy. He didn't have the brut ruggedness of Max, but had plenty of muscles that girls would go crazy for. With his low rise jeans hanging just below his waist as he leaned against the wall, he could be in an ad for Abercrombie and Fitch.

I glanced at Max, who was standing so close I could feel the heat coming off of his body, and automatically shivered with delight. James was handsome, but Max was by far the sweetest eye candy around. James might give me a cavity, but Max would send both of my dentist's kids through college after he'd repaired all the damage.

"Of course you can go James," Cassie giggled. "It wouldn't be the same without you boring me with some story about being a war general or major or whatever you were."

Adam rolled his eyes and held Cassie closer, "Sergeant Major. And I happen to be fascinated by those stories."

"You would," she retorted. "Your stories are almost as boring as his!"

At that, Cassie ducked out of Adam's arms before he could retaliate. He gave her a sly grin that promised she was in for it later. Running out door after her, Adam yelled back to us, "Meet you in fifteen."

Max and James left for their respective rooms. I went into my bathroom and was brushing my teeth when she popped her head back in.

"I love teasing them, they get so serious about their military ranks," she laughed. I smiled around my toothbrush and shook my head. She turned to go back into her own bathroom, but paused. "So I assume you slept well?" she teased, winking and trotted away without waiting for my reply.

I realized at that moment the whole group knew Max and I slept in the same room together and could only imagine what they thought had gone on. I further realized I didn't care. I had no embarrassment about it because I hoped one day he'd be spending all of his nights next to me.

The Commons served a buffet style breakfast and I piled my plate high with French toast, bacon, fresh fruit, and a cherry Danish. Coffee and fresh squeezed orange juice topped off my meal, and I dug in. I hadn't eaten since before the incident (well, other than through a tube) and felt starved. The five of us gathered at a back table so we could have some privacy and talk. Adam and James each had two plates of food and were shoveling it down like it was the last meal on earth while Max was teasing Cassie, a staunch vegetarian, by wiggling a piece bacon in front of her. There was casual conversation about weekend plans and the new iPad James received (hey, we may not be human anymore but we still love all the same toys).

As I carefully picked all of the gross apples from my fruit salad, I sat watching my new friends. I had only known them a short time, but they already felt like my family. I was blessed that they were the ones who had rescued me and comforted to know that they didn't give up on finding me.

Watching my friends laugh and joke around the breakfast table, I resolved I wouldn't let them down. I knew with certainty I was meant to do this job now. I would fight to make sure no one else suffered the way I had. The vampires thought I was their prey – weak and easy to snatch up. They underestimated me. I'd make them regret that mistake. They may have won this small battle, but make no mistake, I would win the war. I was stronger than they realized, and they wouldn't get rid of me so easily. It would take more than a cowardly attack in the dark when I couldn't defend myself. In the end, I would kill the bastards.

Every last one of them.

Sarah M. Ross

Eight

Around noon I was back in the same classroom I started in and pissed about it. After everything that had been done to me, another history lecture was not what I needed. I wanted practical lessons I could actually use. I wanted to train to kill the vampires that tried to kill me. I was done being afraid, and I wouldn't feel sorry for myself anymore. I paced restlessly around the room trying to get a handle on my emotions. If James asked me to sit down, I knew I would explode at him, and he didn't deserve that after helping save me. I took a deep breath and then a second. It didn't seem to do the trick. Maybe after another 6000 deep breaths I'd finally be calm. Max and Cassie both watched me, but I was surprised that it was Adam who spoke up.

"I get it Lucy," His voice was reassuring. "You're frustrated and want to lash out at something or someone. You want to be out there fighting back, and you hate being stuck in here. You're hurt and angry and violated and need an outlet for all those emotions so you think that fighting and killing will make you feel better. Well, I have news for you–it won't. Revenge will not make what happened to you okay and it won't take any of that pain away. Fighting is the smallest part of what we do. In fact, we avoid fighting as much as possible. That's not what being a Patronus is about. We protect."

That was the final drop that sent the water over the dam. "They're attacking us! Why aren't we being proactive and making sure it doesn't happen again? Why am I supposed to be okay with sitting on my ass when there's the chance it could happen to someone else? How is that protecting anyone?"

James stood in the doorway with his arms folded across his chest. "We're not sitting on our asses, Lucy. We're trying to help you so this doesn't happen again. We're going to show you how to make sure it doesn't happen again–to you or anyone else. Do you think we weren't worried sick when we couldn't find you? Don't you think we want to just go out and eliminate every vampire and werewolf that exists simply to make sure no one else ever hurts the way you're hurting right now? We do! But we know that our role is not to avenge or retaliate, as much as we may want to at times. Do you remember why you went into that building to begin with?"

My blood was still boiling, but I knew yelling, kicking, and screaming would get me nowhere. "Yes, I do," I responded softly, hanging my shoulders. I forgot that I never even knew what happened to the other potential victim in the situation.

"You went in searching for Mrs. Kremnik. You knew she was in danger, and you acted. You risked yourself to make sure she was safe because she was innocent. She led a peaceful life and deserved a peaceful afterlife. It was your job to make sure that happened and *it did*."

I let out a deep breath as I heard his last two words.

"She wasn't hurt or turned. She's safe and has already left our realm," James continued.

"But that's not because of me! The only reason she was safe is because that vampire thought he had a better target in me than her! I couldn't do anything to keep her or me safe!" I snapped back at him.

James stepped towards me and put his hands on my shoulders. He sat me down in the closest chair and took the one opposite me. "Lucy, I want to tell you a story. It's not something I like to talk about, but you need to hear it. It will help you understand a little better. About 120 years ago, there was another attack on a new Patronus. Like you, she was also under my care. She had been here for five weeks and was much further along in her training than you are now. One night she was asked to act as a Guide. Guides are another role we fill at times for those who need assistance after their death, usually small children or the mentally impaired. She wasn't supposed to go alone, I was to accompany her but she was eager to prove she was ready for more and begged me to let her try it just once. She was escorting a four year old child who died from influenza. When she arrived back at the doorway, a vampire tried to snatch the child. She fought the vampire to the best of her ability, but within a few minutes she had been drained and the child was taken. I didn't even know she was missing until after it was too late for her. She knew how to attack a vampire and what their weaknesses were. She knew how to keep the child safe with defensive weapons, but she panicked and died because of it."

He stopped for a minute and I had the urge to hug him. I could see a sheen in his eyes and knew he was fighting back tears. "It was my fault. I shouldn't have let her go alone, but she swore she was ready. She wasn't and paid the price for my mistake." He paused again, shaking his head before speaking to me without quavering. "Lucy, you survived with next to no training whatsoever. Your instincts helped you when we failed, again. I know you feel like you didn't do enough, but you're here and that proves you did. I know it is hard for you right now, but I swear to you we are not just sitting back and waiting for attacks. I will teach you how to fight, but there is so much more you need to learn first. You are going to be a great Patronus, but the first lesson you need to learn is patience."

Cassie, Max, and Adam joined us and we sat in silence for a while. The palpable tension in the room had my eyes darting around searching for a way to break it. I didn't want to argue with them. They weren't the source of my frustration. I squeezed my eyes shut and rubbed them for a minute. I knew they were right, but speaking the words out loud was too much at the moment. I, long ago, learned life wasn't fair, and now I was learning that death wasn't either. I stood up and stomped to the front of the room. I needed space to pace and collect my words before I began.

"I'm not mad at you, James, or any of you. I am so grateful that you saved me and even more grateful for being selected to become a Patronus. I am frustrated with myself." I let out a breath I'd apparently been holding. "I can be patient. I just can't be idle. Can you understand that?" I looked at the four of them and searched their eyes, hoping to see tolerance and forgiveness for my tantrum.

I expected James or Max to answer me, but neither did. They didn't get the chance before Cassie jumped up and engulfed me in a bear hug. It lasted far longer than I was ready for and I struggled to breath. She loosened her grip but did not let me go before speaking to me. "Let's get you trained!" It was exactly what I wanted to hear.

The next few weeks flew by in a blur. I worked out or trained during almost all my waking hours. I was sore and exhausted, and I loved it! Being a Patronus made me faster and stronger than when I was human. I still had to work hard to train my body and mind, but it came quicker and easier than it ever would have if I was still human.

I also learned so much from James about our history. I never realized so many famous names throughout history had become Patroni. Joan of Arc, James Dean, and Anne Frank all had breakfast across from me one day! I had to struggle to make sure the food went in my mouth and not on my lap as I unabashedly stared. To say I was star struck would be an understatement!

Adam was brilliant at teaching me maneuvers and techniques, and we spent many hours sparring. He told me one day after pinning me for what I'm sure was the thirtieth time that he had been in the army when he died and a wrestler in school. No wonder he was able to kick my butt three ways from Sunday. But he never went easy on me, and I was thankful for it. He knew he'd have to give me his best in order to train me to be my best. We practiced for so many hours Cassie would have to come in and threaten him with "no lovin" for a month if he didn't get his butt home.

I learned so many things about my bracelet and various ways to detain or seriously injure a vampire. Apparently, a wood stake through the heart was another of the myths vampires started, but intolerance to the sun or UV lights was a very effective tool for warding off a vampire. While I wished I had known that during my time of crisis, I loved absorbing all the new knowledge. James explained that conjuring a flashlight with UV bulbs, like in a tanning bed, could actually catch a vampire on fire! I practiced on an outdoor course with sand traps, mud pits, a rock wall and zip lines repeatedly. It had dummy vampires that would jump out and attack, but I was able to easily restrain them in seconds before moving on. I was improving my time daily and James happily announced in front of the whole Commons one night that I beat the previous record for new recruits on the timed course!

Cassie worked out at the gym or went on long runs with me every day and kept my mind off of my previous trauma with gossip about who was seeing who and stories from when she was alive. She never ceased to amaze me with her stories about secretly starting an underground feminist movement when she was sixteen or helping slaves escape when she was only ten. At night, we would watch old episodes of Mystery Science Theater 3000 and laugh until we hurt, or challenge James and Adam to games of pool. We would hustle them so they had to make us ice cream sundaes with extra whipped cream and cherries. I never laughed harder than when Adam tried to smash a dollop of whipped cream on Cassie's face only to realize too late she had the whole can behind her back, and she made him a whipped cream hat!

    I was finally getting into a great groove with my new friends and finding purpose in my afterlife. I was happy for the first time since I died. Only one thing could have made things better: Max. A few days after I began my new training regimen he sort of disappeared. He never came to the training center or ate with us in the Commons. The absence was suspicious. He didn't join us for movies or pool either. He just was never around. I saw glimpses of him coming or going every once in a while, but he would quickly keep moving when I spotted him. I went to his room once after I saw him get in the elevator, but even though I knocked and knocked he wouldn't answer it. Not seeing him or being with him left me feeling empty, like I was missing a limb. He had been there every day since I came into this world, and the void left in his absence was painful. I tried to ask James, but he abruptly changed the topic each time I asked. I wondered if I was the cause of his sudden disappearing act. Had I upset him somehow…

    "You're awfully quiet today," Cassie mused as we passed mile ten in our run.

    "Actually, there's something I wanted to ask you about." I started, not breaking stride. "Is Max mad at me? Did I do something to offend him?"

    Cassie glanced in my direction but didn't slow her pace. "Why would you think such a thing?"

    "Because of his sudden Houdini act," I explained. "Why else would he just abruptly stop hanging around or talking to me?"

"I can honestly tell you that it's not you, it's him," she replied, but there was no confidence in her tone.

I snorted at the cheesy line and wondered why she was defending him.

She continued, "I swear it to you. He said he's been working on a project. I have no idea what, but he asked James to reassign him for a month or two. None of us have seen him any more than you have. I only know this because he told Adam one night when I was over there."

"Why would he do that? Don't you find it a tad odd that after I join the team he asks to be reassigned?" It was too big of a coincidence. It had to be because of me. I thought he liked me, and I thought, maybe, he might even ask me out after the night we spent together. Was I wrong? Was I so off base that I was imagining he liked me when really he couldn't wait to get away from me? I felt like there was a boulder in the pit of my stomach and suddenly I couldn't keep running. I stopped by a bench and began to stretch my legs while attempting not to cry. Okay, so he didn't like me. It's not like we had been in love or dated or anything. He was just like any other guy. I would ignore it and keep working. It was no big deal. So why did I feel like my heart was ripped in two and shoved down a garbage disposal?

"Go talk to him," she said softly. I focused on her with tears welling in my eyes and couldn't say anything. I knew that one syllable out of my mouth would release the floodgates, and I needed to be stronger than that. She gave me a quick hug and took off running again. I sat down on the bench, trying to understand my emotions. Why was I so upset about a guy not liking me after only having spent a few days with him? Why did I feel physical pain at being separated from him for a few weeks? This was crazy! I was better than this weepy girl sitting on a bench sulking. I shook my head vigorously and stood up. No, I wouldn't talk to him. If he wanted to avoid me, fine. I wouldn't let him have that much power over me. Training–that's what I needed to be focused on. I took off running back towards the training center and hoped to find James or Adam. I needed a good sparring match right now. I just hoped I wouldn't hurt them too badly.

I jogged back from where we came. When I rounded the corner to the entrance of the training complex, I skidded to a stop. Max was leaning against the entrance doors and if I wanted to go inside, I'd have to pass by him. I took a deep breath and squared my shoulders. I would simply walk by. It wouldn't be painful at all. I tried to convince myself repeatedly while knowing full well I was failing. I marched toward the doors and avoided eye contact, knowing that one look into his perfect blue eyes would be my undoing. I was almost passed him when he reached out and took my arm. I yelped in surprise and stumbled over my feet, sending my body crashing to the ground. Max was instantly at my side trying to help me up. The feel of his warm skin on mine sent a series of goosebumps down my arms and I cursed my body's betrayal.

"Are you okay Lucy?" He fretted, concern evident in his voice.

"Fine," I said tersely. I wanted to go inside where it wouldn't be so painful, but Max still had a hold of my arm and placed his other around my waist to help me up. I tried to break free of his hold but he didn't allow it.

"I'm fine, you can let go now." I tried as an attempt to break the physical contact even as my body screamed for me not to leave his side.

"Actually, I was waiting for you. I wanted to talk to you," he explained. My eyes betrayed my curiosity and longing, and he smiled. "There's something I've been meaning to tell you, but haven't found the right time before now. Can we go somewhere to talk?" he asked politely.

I wanted nothing more than to scream *yes*, but was too fearful of what he had to say. I was convinced he would explain he found another team with someone better than me, and he was leaving forever. Who was I trying to kid? He was way too attractive to like someone as simple and plain as me. His hands were still holding me up and I involuntarily sucked a breath in and greedily swallowed his rich, musky scent–allowing myself to be engulfed in it. It was my undoing. I had no will power to say no as every molecule in my body craved to be near him. I could hear the rational part of my brain begging me to be cautious, but its voice was quiet against the overwhelming roar of satisfaction I received from him touching me.

    I had only been away from him for a few weeks, but it was like giving water to a person who'd been stranded in the hottest desert for months. Having just his fingers lightly touching the crook of my arm gave me a sense of completeness I didn't even know I was missing. I knew that I missed him, but not how much needed him, or craved him as much as I did until now. How could I have been so blind to what was so obvious? It would have been like Mozart not realizing he missed music or Babe Ruth not realizing he missed playing baseball. I shook my head a few times to clear my thoughts. I may want to be near him, but he obviously didn't feel the same way. I staggered back to gain some distance between him and myself. I didn't have to go far because at that moment, James opened the door to the training complex and faced each of us.

    "Good, I'm glad you're both here. Let's step inside, shall we?" James beckoned. I peered at him questioningly, but he didn't give me time to ask why. He turned right back around and went inside, leaving Max and I no choice but to do the same. Max held the door open for me, following James into a small conference room where we took seats across from each other. James didn't join us, but told us to hold on for a minute while he walked back towards the front. I kept my eyes down and began tapping my foot up and down rapidly, not comfortable with the distance between us both. I wanted to be closer and farther away at the same time. After a few minutes, Cassie and Adam joined James and came inside the room. They all uncomfortably took seats around the table. I scanned the room, waiting for someone to explain what was going on.

Cassie looked pensive as she played with strands of her hair. I could tell she was nervous, but I wasn't sure what she had to be nervous about. James took his usual stance leaning against the door with his arms folded, and Adam rubbed Cassie's back. What in the world was going on here? I gave everyone a few more seconds before audibly groaning.

"Is someone going to say something or are we going to sit here all day?" I grumbled.

"Okay, okay," Cassie conceded and sat more upright in her seat. "I'll tell you what I know, but I really don't think I'm the person you should be asking. It really should be Max." She looked ashamed now, but I didn't understand why. What would she have to be ashamed about?

"Max, I agree. I think you need to explain a couple of things to Lucy. Starting with where you've been recently," Adam chimed in. For Adam to voice his opinion at all told me it must be serious. I sought Max's face and he nodded once in affirmation. His face was suddenly serious, and I knew what he was about to say was not going to be good news.

"I had been meaning to talk to you for a few days, but I was too chicken to actually face you," Max admitted.

"Why were you scared to talk to me?" I started to ask, but stopped. I wouldn't allow my voice to betray how hurt I was at his absence.

"I didn't ask to be reassigned because I wanted to be away from you, Lucy. Please don't think that; it's the furthest thing from the truth! I have never been happier than since you joined us. Trust me on that."

"Then I don't get it," I pouted. "If my being on the team made you happy, why did you ask to leave as soon as I joined?"

"Okay. You know I asked to be reassigned for a month. Well I was working on an independent project of sorts." Max settled into the chair across from me but wasn't meeting my eyes. This was worse than I thought. "I got word from a friend–an angel friend who works for the Alpha. He let me know that I needed to be prepared for an upcoming… event." I narrowed my eyes in confusion, trying to make sense of what he was telling me.

"I don't get it. What is the event?" This whole conversation had me feeling like I was watching an old episode of Lost–ending with more questions than when it started.

"It involves you. He knew I was on your team and might be able to help you through it." Max was visibly upset and was barely whispering the words now, like if he said them softly they wouldn't have as much of an impact.

"Max, just spit it out. Whatever it is I can see that it's upsetting you. What kind of event would concern me, and why would an angel from the Alpha be involved?"

"Okay, let me back up and explain a few things first." He took a deep breath and glanced at Cassie for support. She was pulling and twisting at strands of her hair and looking down at her feet. She was clearly not getting involved. "Do you remember James telling you about the role of Guides in our realm?"

"Yes…" I answered, unsure where this was going.

"Well, let me explain in a little more detail. Guides are members of our teams that specifically just transport. They don't stay on this realm and protect, they just go between worlds. Think of them as flight attendants, always zipping from one assignment to the next. Since they're transporting people who need help, they can't wait until the person has actually died before going there. They need to arrive before hand. You can imagine what might happen if a small child dies and no one is there waiting for them—the confusion they would feel and how easily they could wander off." I nodded in agreement, but didn't say anything, wanting him to continue. "There are some angels of the Alpha whose job it is to determine when it's time for Guides to be prepared. They do the scheduling you could say. Sometimes, with up to a several weeks notice of where and when a Guide will be needed to make sure someone's available. My friend, Marco, is one of those angels. He had a special assignment he thought I should handle instead of one of the usual Guides."

At his last words, it clicked, and I felt my heart drop to the farthest pit of my stomach. "It's Jessica, isn't it?" I whispered. Looking at Max now, the pain on his face was all I needed to know that my words were true. I jumped out of my seat and began to scream.

"NO! No, No, No, No!" I shook my head vigorously in denial. "It's not fair! She's only eleven! Please not Jessica!!" I begged. Both he and Cassie stood up and embraced me. I was glad they were there, because if I had not had them holding me up I would have crumbled to the ground. I continued my mutterings and pleadings of, "No, not Jessica" and put my arms around Max, needing to feel his strength now that I had none. "Please no, *please*. My parents can't handle losing another child. She's only eleven! She hasn't had a chance to live yet! Please Max, *please!*"

"I'm so sorry, Lucy. I'm so sorry," he said, soothing me while rubbing my back. It eased some of the ache I felt, but I couldn't let myself become soft.

Suddenly, I pushed away from him and Cassie. "When?" I demanded. I would be strong for my sister, even if it's the last thing I could do for her. Even if it killed me to do it.

"Marco gave me warning, letting me know her condition has gotten worse," he divulged before adding quietly, "and wouldn't be getting better. It could be a day or another week. He said he'd let me know as the time came."

"But you asked to be reassigned weeks ago! You've known all this time and didn't say anything to me?" I was furious. I couldn't believe he didn't come to me as soon as he heard.

"I'm sorry. I was trying to help, a desperate Hail Mary to prevent this," he admitted.

"What kind of Hail Mary? Is there something I can do to prevent this?" Hope suddenly soared inside me.

"I went to the Council for the Alpha and Omega asking them for a reevaluation. They didn't grant my request. I'm sorry; I pulled every string I had."

"So that's it. There's no hope for her now?" I sobbed. I balled my fists and felt my nails digging into my palms—the small physical pain was comforting somehow.

"The decision was final."

Cassie handed me some tissues and I blotted my eyes. It was amazing how I could feel so good one moment and in the next have my heart ripped out and handed to me. I hated feeling helpless and needed to do something. "I will be her Guide." I stated firmly to Max. "Tell Marco that I will be the one escorting my sister."

"I'm sorry, Lucy, I can't do that. He's already bending the rules to let me do it. You're too new. It's not safe."

"I *am* going." I threw back at him. "It will be ME!"

"Lucy, no one doubts that you could do this," Cassie stated, still using a soothing tone to try to assuage my anger and grief. "You're by far the strongest recruit we've had in generations. You're just too emotionally tied to this. Your emotions— not your strength— could be what gets you hurt."

"Maybe you're not hearing me," I seethed through clenched teeth. "If my sister—my *baby* sister—is going to die and leave my parents with both of their children dead, then it's going to be *me* who is there when it happens. Not anyone else. It will be my face my sister sees when her spirit leaves her body. I will be the one to make sure she knows it's okay, and she's going to be safe. I will be the one to comfort her as she blames herself for leaving my parents with no one!"

I paced the room, searching for something to punch. I needed to release my grief and I was suddenly claustrophobic in this room. I needed out. I needed to run. I brushed by Max and Cassie, knocking her down in the process. I didn't stop to apologize; I just took off for the trails behind the series of offices and complexes. I pulled off my sweater and threw it on one of the still empty benches and blasted through the doors. Amazingly, I was not crying anymore about the news I'd received. I was too angry to be upset. I ran by the training building and knocked over a trash can in my way. It felt good kicking it, and I embraced the pain I now felt in my knee and toes. I needed pain. I needed have the physical pain to dull the emotional pain.

I ran and enjoyed the burning in my lungs and pushed myself to go faster. I heard my name being called from a distance, but I wouldn't slow down to let them catch up. I needed to think, and I needed to be alone to do it. I found myself in a heavily wooded section of the grounds I'd not explored before and no longer had a trail to follow. No matter, I would make my own. I pushed myself, even as I could feel the bushes and trees scraping against my skin as I cut a new path. I knew I was probably bleeding, but I didn't care. I just needed to feel the burning in my legs and not think about anything else.

An ominous noise next to me brought me to a halt, and I turned to my right. There, hiding in the bushes was a vampire, snarling and baring its fangs ready to attack. I scanned the area, wondering why no alarms had been set off with the arrival of the creature. The smell of my fresh blood must have drawn him out of hiding. Good—this was exactly the fight I was looking for. I stood staring at it for a moment, but he didn't make a move. I could see he was a younger vampire than the last who attacked me, but that wouldn't matter.

"Well what are you waiting for?" I yelled. I had no patience for games today. The vampire's lips curled and it sprung at me, unable to resist the scent of fresh blood any longer. I stepped back, using my bracelet to conjure up silver gloves. When the vampire was close enough, I punched him—hard. He howled in pain as the skin melted off of his arm and throat where I grabbed him. I did not let up on my assault and conjured four silver stakes. I jammed one in each arm and leg rendering him immobile. The vampire tried to lift its arms to release them, but the silver went all the way through and held him down like tent poles. I stood up and glared down at my would-be attacker.

"Today is the wrong day to pick a fight with me," I seethed. The vampire spit at me and growled but didn't reply. "You think you can kill me—on my turf?" I kicked the vampire with my newly added silver toe boots. I could smell the rotten stench of his burning flesh as it soured in the back of my throat and stirred up bile, but it did not deter me. I kicked at him again and he let out a high-pitched scream. The scream startled me and I squinted at the vampire only to realize it was a boy of no more than fifteen. I instinctively felt bad about my attack and moved away, but only for a second. I realized that this teenage boy would have easily tried to kill me like any other vampire. I produced a UV flashlight from my bracelet and turned it on, shining it just above the vampire so he knew what was coming. I gradually aimed the beam towards him, shining it on his fingertips and pulling back, watching them ignite. I then aimed it on his toes and repeated the process. I began to aim for his eyes, but just then Max and Cassie caught up with me. They took in the scene and rushed over to me.

"What the hell is this?" Max scolded, clearly disturbed by what he saw. Cassie scouted the area to make sure there were no other vampires hiding out. I hadn't been thinking! I should have done that as soon as I had the vampire secure with the poles.

"I found a vampire," I answered calmly, "Or rather, it found me. Tried to attack me so I defended myself." I shrugged my shoulders nonchalantly.

"And was torture included in your defense?" Max chided, disappointment so clear in his eyes that I mentally re-evaluated my actions.

"I just... It's just that..." I stammered. He was right. I had gone too far and I knew that wasn't right. Max grimaced as I faced what I'd done. "No, you're right. I went too far and took out my anger in the wrong way. I'm so sorry." His lips drew into a straight line and I knew he hated what I had done, but a momentary softness in his eyes told me he wouldn't stay mad.

"Just finish it so we can talk please," he sighed. I knew he was disappointed by my actions and even angry with me. It hurt me when I realized this and I was suddenly disgusted with myself.

I nodded my head and approached the vampire. He struggled more against the binds now that he knew his final fate was approaching. I used my bracelet to conjure the only weapon that could successfully kill a vampire— a fully silver syringe-like object that when injected directly into the heart can suck the stolen soul into it, thus killing the vampire. Since vampires are created by stealing souls, stealing them back (or sucking them out as the case may be) was the only way to destroy one.

Once done, the remains shriveled and would soon be nothing but ash. Cassie searched the pockets of the clothes it was wearing for any identification or clues to give our Research department. She found a driver's license with the name "Andrew Simmons" on it and showed his age as sixteen. Max didn't move but continued to stare at me as I picked up the syringe and placed the cap back on it.

"I'll take him to the Retrieval team and give you some time to talk," Cassie noted, trotting off in the direction I'd come.

Left alone with Max now, I didn't know where to start. First, he disappeared for almost three weeks only to return to tell me my sister was dying. Then I ran out and tortured a vampire. To say our relationship had become complicated would be an understatement. And that was before the inexplicable feelings I had for him were factored in. I didn't know where to begin our conversation, so I let him take the lead. We trudged back sluggishly, neither of us speaking. I focused on the sounds of the leaves and twigs crunching below my feet as we walked. I actively tried not to think of Jessica or my parents now; I wasn't ready to tackle that yet.

I kept my gaze down; I had too much shame at what I'd just done to meet Max's eyes. I focused on my steps, carefully stepping over rocks and fallen branches. I hadn't noticed any of this on my frenzied run in, but the beauty that surrounded me now could not be ignored. Green vines twined up trees and delicate flowers blossomed in bright yellows, pinks, and reds. I never thought I'd see sights such as these again and felt gratitude that someone had the foresight to add them to our realm. Jessica would have loved this, I absently thought to myself. She was always the outdoorsy girl—active in Girl Scouts and Brownies. She loved camping and went on week long trips with our grandparents each summer. I always opted out of them, claiming a busy sports schedule, but really I just wanted her to get to have them to herself for a bit. She'd always tried to impress them by announcing the names of all of the varieties of flora she knew.

Tears were now silently rolling down my cheeks. Max noticed, but didn't try to comfort me. Nothing could at this point. I would have to get through this on my own as much as my friends wanted to help.

We reached the edge of the wooded area and paused. Max took my hand and gave it a small tug, urging me to follow him. We continued to a gazebo at the back of the meadow where the spirits lingered. No one else was occupying it, so we stepped inside and I took a seat. I smiled at the spirits that meandered around, out for a stroll or playing chess nearby. No one stopped to talk to us, and I was grateful. Words were lost for me now.

"You ready to talk about this?" Max broke in after a time.

"Can you ever be ready?" I tossed back.

He didn't respond but sat pondering for a few seconds. "Do you remember how I told you my death was too painful to talk about?" he started.

"Of course."

"I want to tell you a little about it now." He started as I turned towards him, "As I told you, I was 22 when I died. I had been out at the theatre with my wife and we'd left our infant son at home. It was the first time both of us had been away from him at the same time since he was born. We left him with a neighbor girl who lived in a farm down the road. Beth Ann attended our church with her parents, and we'd known her for several years. She was older than the other girls in our area and even though she was a little quirky, we thought that her age made her more suited to watch Nathanial than the others in the neighborhood. When we arrived home, she stabbed my wife as soon as she walked in the door. She never had a chance and bled out in minutes. I tried to help her rather than apprehend the girl—a mistake. The girl came up behind me and stabbed me too. I watched helplessly as she scooped up Nathanial and strode out the door with him. I couldn't save my wife, and I couldn't save my son. It took me hours to die. And in each minute of those last few hours I knew it was my fault and screamed out, cursing the gods at the unfairness of it all. My son and wife were innocent. They did not deserve the fate they received. I was not mad about my own death; it seemed a fitting punishment for the crime of not protecting them."

My heart broke for him as he told me his story. I no longer felt jealous he had loved another, but swelled with empathy for him. "Oh Max..."

"After making my transition to a Patronus, James told me what happened. I forced him to, not ready to let go and needing any scrap of information he found to hold on to my grief. It turned out the girl had miscarried several times before and saw Nathanial as her only chance to have a child of her own. But life on the run without money or support proved too much for her. She became sick and died after a few years, leaving Nathanial on the steps of a nunnery just before her death.

"The reason I'm telling you my story is not for you to feel bad for me. I want to show you what holding on to your past and not accepting the deaths of your loved ones can do to you. It made me crazy for many years. I don't want that for you. Eventually everyone you know and love is going to pass on. You may see them here or just hear about it later, but everyone will die. It's the only downside to immortality."

He stood up, walked towards me, and knelt, taking my hands in his. "Life sucks, Lucy."

I smiled at his comment and he continued, "But afterlife doesn't. It can be amazing if you let it. The sense of purpose, pride, and accomplishment are worth the pain. I always felt that teaching was the most rewarding profession, but it's got nothing on this job. Please, don't make the same mistakes I did and wallow in misery for the next fifty years."

I knew he was right and knew I should follow his advice, but it was hard. Letting go of the one person who made me smile the most as a human seemed like an impossibility. I wanted to protect her now and couldn't. He must have known that too because he gave me a gift to make it a little easier.

"I've thought about it," he started, "and I'm going to let you come with me to help act as Guide for your sister. You're not going alone, but you can come with me, and we can do it together. I'll have to clear it with James, but he should be agreeable to this compromise."

I threw my arms around him, "Thank you, thank you, thank you," I squealed.

"It'll help you have closure and heal faster." He hugged me in return. "It will give you what I never got."

I didn't answer, but kept my arms around him, squeezing him tightly, both in thanks for what he gave me and in sympathy for what had happened to him. He leaned back, and I let go. Smiling, he told me we needed to go to James and then to Marco. Without the approval of both, I couldn't go.

James proved the easier of the two. He listened as Max explained his rationale behind having me go. The men argued for what seemed like hours, each producing reason after reason why I should or should not go. I let Max argue my case, using his experiences to sway James. Finally, after muttered curses under his breath about going all in with pocket deuces, he agreed. I kissed his cheek in thanks, trying not to squeal in delight, and we set off to see Marco.

Nine

The next day, after much needed sleep, we set off to see Marco the angel.

"What's he like?" I whispered to Max. "I've never met an angel before. Are they like us or are they all in white with wings? Do they sit on clouds all day playing the harp?"

Max snorted loudly at the suggestion. "No wings," he explained. "And they don't dress in all white. They're much like us but since they were never human they don't look exactly the same. For example, their skin is more iridescent and their eyes are entirely silver. They look like pools of liquid mercury."

"Freaky!"

"Just don't say that when you meet Marco. One more thing you should know is that they can hear your thoughts. So be careful what you think and say around him."

"Seriously? How cool is that!" I exclaimed.

"Yeah, real cool until they hear your most embarrassing moments and then tease you mercilessly for the next century," Max muttered offhandedly.

"Oh, I guess that would be bad. What embarrassing secret does Marco have on you?" I teased. This was taking my mind off of why where were going there in the first place, and I relished the distraction.

"Sorry, not telling you," Max declared.

"C'mon! Just a hint".

"Never going to happen!"

I pushed out my bottom lip in a pout and gave him my best sad face. It almost worked and I could see his resolve crumbling, but then we reached the door that would take us to Marco's office and he changed the subject.

"Okay, this is it. When we get in there, let me do the talking. He'll try to hear your thoughts anyway, but stay focused on Jessica. If you think about her enough, he'll see that it's what you need for closure," Max instructed.

"Not a problem. I've been consumed by thoughts of Jessica since you told me," I answered. I spent hours last night going through old picture albums I had of Jessica and watching home movies. Cassie was amazing enough to get these for me—Lord only knows how— and I cried and smiled and laughed as I watched them.

Max took my hand, giving it a small squeeze as he led me towards a large blue door that was at least ten feet high. We strode through side by side, and it felt like being sucked out into space. Everything went black, and I felt like I was falling and being pushed pulled at the same time. The pressure on my newly healed bones was indescribable. I clenched my teeth as pain ripped through my newly healed body, but it only lasted a minute. Before I knew it, I was standing in what appeared to be a waiting room, and Max was at my side. I immediately turned and vomited in the closest trash can.

"What was *that*?" I cried, wiping my mouth and wishing I had some gum.

"We changed realms. Angels aren't based on our realm; they have their own closer to the Alpha." Max handed me a tissue and looked very concerned for just a moment.

"Little warning next time maybe?" I smirked.

"Whoops. Guess I forgot you haven't done any traveling since you started. I'm really sorry, Lucy."

"Didn't really have the time what with being attacked and almost dying and all," I snorted. Max cringed at the memory, and I quickly changed the subject, knowing he still harbored some unnecessary guilt over the incident. I surveyed the small room. It had several metal folding chairs against one wall and a small card table containing a half empty coffee pot and an assortment of pink, blue, and yellow sweetener packets sprawled across it. On a wobbly coffee table sat an array of magazines dating back to the 1980s, judging by the teased hair and pegged jeans of the models on the covers. There were similar blue doors on three of the walls and a black door on the fourth. We took a seat in two of the chairs, and I tried to glance inconspicuously at the other people there. There were four other people in the room besides us and none looked startled by our entrance or my vomiting, so I assumed it's pretty common. A freakishly tall creature with gray horns was pouring himself a cup of coffee while a petite woman with shimmering wings read an old edition of Cosmo. The other two people had the iridescent skin that Max had previously told me about, and I purposefully avoided staring at them.

"So where exactly are we now?"

"We're in Marco's office—technically his waiting room. He keeps several appointments a day and is squeezing us in, so be grateful. Usually he's booked weeks in advance."

"I'm eternally grateful, trust me!" I promised. Suddenly feeling parched, I spied a completely empty water cooler that had obviously not been filled in quite some time and crossed my legs, trying to keep my butt from falling asleep in the hard chair. I wondered why everything looked so dumpy and decided to ask Max, but chose my words carefully as to not insult anyone. "He sure doesn't keep the most modern of waiting rooms though does he?"

The two iridescent people snickered before Max could reply, "Remember to watch your thoughts!"

I cringed, realizing that they knew what I was really thinking and could have kicked myself. I couldn't afford to get on Marco's bad side.

Max just rubbed his thumb over my palm and whispered in my ear, "He does it on purpose. Comfortable people stay and linger. Comfortable people make multiple appointments, and ask for favors." I enjoyed the brief touch of the edge of his lips on the tip of my ear as he spoke and felt my heart flutter.

"Ohhh, I see," I whispered back, knowing it was pointless if people could just read my thoughts anyway. I resolved myself to concentrate and spent the next ten minutes thinking only of Jessica. Well, her and Max as he continued to gently rub the back of my palm soothingly as he held my hand.

The black inner door opened and a short, thin man wearing a charcoal grey three piece pinstripe suit came out. He looked like he could work on Wall Street with red power tie and perfectly shined wingtip shoes. Max stood and began walking toward him, and I followed his lead.

"Marco! Thanks so much for meeting with us today," Max greeted him, reaching out to shake Marco's bony hand. "This is Lucy. Lucy, this is Marco."

"Pleased to meet you," I addressed. "Thank you so much for seeing us." I tried actively to think of Jessica and ignored the urges to stare at him. He was several inches shorter than me with long blonde hair to his waist that was tied in a braid. His sharp angular face set off his liquid silver eyes in a way that wouldn't be believed unless seen and I was glad that Max warned me in advance. He was gaunt and had very pointed features that reminded me of what I'd pictured a goblin to look like. He was the most un-angelic person I could have imagined. He held my gaze for several stiff moments, then at Max, and back at me.

"Interesting," he mused, smiling slyly.

My eyes squinted in obvious confusion and I glanced at Max, hoping he had some idea what was going on. Max didn't say anything but the look on his face said he knew what Marco was implying and he wasn't amused.

"And she doesn't know?" Marco commented, directing the question at Max. Okay, now I was totally lost.

"We're here to discuss Lucy assisting me in Guide duties for her sister, Jessica," Max reminded him sternly. "That's *all* we're here to discuss."

That certainly spiked my curiosity, and Marco must have read my thoughts. I didn't want him to have any excuse to say no to our request so I tabled them and went back to thinking of Jessica. Nothing was more important than that. Marco kept smiling, but I held firm.

"Please, step into my office," he requested, gesturing and leading us inside a small windowless room. It was filled floor to ceiling with bookshelves made from dark cherry wood and a few overgrown ferns surrounding a standing black onyx and silver globe that was sitting in the corner. An oversized desk in the same dark wood sat in the middle of the room with a tall wing back chair behind it. Max sat down in a stiff black chair, and I took the matching one beside it. I shifted nervously, crossing and uncrossing my ankles trying to get comfortable.

"I understand why you've come today Lucy. I just don't believe it's a good idea to send someone as new as you into the field yet," Marco said, getting right to the point.

"I can do this," I stated, holding my resolve firm. "More than that, I need to do this. And I won't be alone— Max will be with me. Between the two of us, I'm confident we can Guide my sister without any problems."

"I know from your thoughts you're unaware of the chatter that's been detected by some of our field agents over the last few weeks. Vampires are talking about the new Patronus who's killed two of them within her first month of training. They're worried and looking for revenge. More than that, they need to take you out to make sure these events don't repeat themselves," Marco informed me. I felt proud and petrified at the same time. "Sending you in the field would be too dangerous for your sister."

"Then add another team member! James or Cassie or anyone else of your choosing— just let me go along so I can be there for my sister," I begged.

"You don't seem to be grasping the point," he said calmly. "You are the problem. The solution is making sure you aren't there. It's the best way to ensure a safe transfer of the spirit."

I fought back tears as I tried to figure out how to convince him I needed this and that it truly would be best for Jessica. I decided to use his mind reading abilities to my advantage. I pulled out every memory I had of Jessica: helping her hide the first tooth she ever lost, taking her to the beach for the first time and building sandcastles with her, holding her hand throughout her first Chemo treatment, helping her write her letter to Santa asking only to be cured, letting her sneak in my room at night and sleep with me after she had a nightmare, sharing a pint of Chocolate Chocolate-chip ice cream while watching The Lion King for the 150th time, and anything else that could show him just how important she was to me. I saw the edge of his mouth twitch, and I knew I was getting through to him.

"Do you see? Can you understand why I need this?" I pleaded.

"While I empathize with your situation, this is no different than the thousands of others who lose a young family member. I am forced to do it every day. Each person has loved ones with memories just like yours, Lucy."

I felt defeated; there was nothing left to do now. I hung my head and stared at my feet, unable to face either Marco or Max. I nodded and resisted the urge to mumble "thanks for nothing" knowing the mind-reading angel would hear me. Before I started to get out of my seat, Marco's words stopped me dead in my tracks.

"But I will grant this– on certain conditions."

I jumped out of my seat in excitement. "Did you just say yes? I'll follow whatever conditions you impose on me.

Anything, I promise," I squealed, looking for Max to confirm I wasn't hallucinating or something.

"Marco, what are the conditions? You're not suggesting?" Max asked, crossing his arms over his chest and glaring down at the angel.

"If she wants to do this, yes."

"You are basically setting her up to fail. You know that Marco."

"Not necessarily. She could pass."

"If you didn't want her to go, you should have just told her no. These conditions are impossible to meet and you know it. You're getting her hopes up for nothing, and it's cruel."

"I'm so sorry you have so little faith in her. I thought you, of all people, would think she could do anything."

"Damn it Marco, stop playing these games," Max yelled, running his fingers through his hair in frustration.

"Okay, that's enough you two. What exactly is so impossible that I have no chance of succeeding?" I interjected.

"You must receive training as a Guide. And pass the certification test which will be given by the head instructor."

Max's eyes held such pity that I knew he meant it was going to be next to impossible. I could pass a test; I could do almost anything if it meant Guiding my sister.

"That's fine. I'll do it," I stated confidently and put out my hand to shake Marco's. He didn't move, but continued to focus on Max.

"Lucy, I don't think you quite know what you're getting yourself into. Maybe you should listen to Max before agreeing so hastily."

Max didn't say anything and continued staring at the angel. Finally, he turned away from Marco and gave me a brief hug. "You can do it Lucy. It'll be fine. I'll make sure of it."

I wasn't quite sure what Max meant, but it didn't matter so long as the end result was me being there for Jessica. We started for the office door to go back to our realm but Marco stopped us with one final statement.

"Three days from now," he stated simply. "I'll send you the final details 24 hours prior to your departure."

Just as suddenly as my joy came, it was taken away. My sister only had three days left to live. My parents would have to face life with two dead children in seventy two hours. Max put his arm back around my waist and addressed Marco, "Understood."

We walked out of his office and through the waiting room to the Realm transport door.

Ten

I spent the next twenty four hours in the training facility with James and Adam. They decided that the "extra training" I needed was to beat me mercilessly— repeatedly. And this was before I even met the head trainer of the Guides. I wasn't sure if they were trying to prove I wasn't ready so I'd back down or trying to beat me unconscious so I couldn't go at all. I'd been punched, kicked, hit, tossed, smacked, and bitten once (though I'm pretty sure that last one was an accident). Through it all, I never stopped. I would get right back up and tell them, "Thank you, may I have another?" just like in boot camp—and in my case during pledging of my sorority. I knew they had my best interest at heart and even though I was exhausted and hurt all over, I kept going. It was what Jessica needed.

I headed over to the water fountain to refuel when Cassie came in. She walked straight towards me and ignored the two shirtless men dripping sweat in the center of the room.

"Luc– you ready for a break?" she inquired wagging a brown paper bag at me.

"Can't. I need to keep training. Time is running out."

"You can afford to stop for ten minutes. Look, I brought you a sandwich," she beamed down at me.

Adam sauntered over when Cassie pulled out the sandwich. "Oh thanks, baby! You brought me lunch!" he said taking the sandwich from her hands and giving her a peck on the cheek. Cassie snatched it right back from him and slapped his hand.

"Absolutely not, Adam! This is for Lucy. Go make your own sandwich if you're hungry. Besides, I want to talk to Lucy alone for a few minutes." She took my arm and led me to the women's locker room knowing Adam and James were unlikely to follow. "Good, we're alone now." She took a seat on the bench between a set of lockers. She patted the spot next to her with her hand urging me to sit as well.

"What's up, Cass? What do you need to talk about that's so urgent?" I said between bites. I really was hungry after all. I finished the entire BLT in about four bites and looked inside the bag to see if she had another one. Thankfully, she did– and there was a bag of Salt & Vinegar chips! Score!

"I'm worried about you. You're acting like you've got everything under control, and I'm concerned you're going to break down eventually. I think you should talk about how you feel about this whole thing. I want to help you."

"I really appreciate the sentiment, Cassie, and the lunch," I insisted between bites, covering my mouth to make sure no food accidentally fell out. "But really, I'm fine. I just need to keep training so I can be prepared in case something goes wrong. I don't want my sister to be hurt."

"Are you worried about the threats Marco told you about?"

"Yes and no. I don't think that anyone will attack us on this mission because no one really knows who I am, so they won't know who my sister is. At the same time, I'm not taking any chances and am doing everything in my power to prepare for every contingency," I explained.

"Lucy, that other vampire was here for three weeks before you found and killed him. Who knows how much information he was able to gather and report back during that time. You can't assume they don't know who you are! That's very dangerous!"

"I don't think he was reporting back. Someone would have seen him sneaking in and out, especially once we beefed up security at the realm doors. Plus, he was dirty and malnourished. If he had gone back to earth, he would have eaten something while there." I stood up, wondering where I left my sports bottle so I could take a few sips after polishing off the chips.

"I see your point" Cassie sighed, starting to give in. "But I still think you need to talk to someone. Have you been talking to Max at least?"

"He's disappeared again," I grumbled, not liking being reminded. I closed my eyes trying to push the thoughts away. When we first got back to this realm, I thought things were going to be better. He joined me until the training center but stopped before coming inside. When I asked him where he was going, he gave me a vague answer about "needing to get a few things ready" and took off. I assumed it had to do with the big tests Marco mentioned, but not having Max around to help with my training hurt. The worst part was I couldn't even tell him how much it hurt. My only consolation was he gave me a hug before leaving. And not just a regular hug, but an embrace. We held on to each other tightly for several minutes, him running his fingers in my hair and me squeezing him tight. Our relationship was so complicated. One minute I thought he really liked me and we would share a great moment. The next, he'd disappear for days. I just couldn't figure him out. I was so irritated at myself for not being more in control of the situation. I needed to talk to him about this, but who knew when he'd make another appearance in my life. Cassie's voice brought me back out of my thoughts.

"...that's why I really believe that not keeping your emotions bottled up is so important. Do you see what I mean now?" she asked. I hadn't heard a word she'd said while I thought back to my last moments with Max, so I just nodded. I was not being a good friend. Here she was trying to help me, and I wasn't even paying attention to her. I promised myself I'd make a better effort after this was all over.

"There's one more thing I want to warn you about, Luc," Cassie continued, "The trainer you're supposed to meet with is on her way. The one Marco told you about."

"Yeah, I heard she was a hard-ass," I teased, but Cassie's face was dead serious.

"You need to brace yourself for her. She makes Marine drill sergeants look like Mary Poppins! You've got to suck up whatever she throws your way and not take any of it personally. She is the key to you passing these tests, and it's going to be hard. Really hard. She can have more mood swings than a pregnant woman. I thought about being a Guide when I first got here and went into the training program. After two days I ran away crying and spent a week in bed feeling like the lowest form of life possible. She has a way of doing that to you, but just remember she's not purposefully trying to make you fail, even if it seems that way. She just has really high standards that pretty much no one can meet."

After the fear of God was put into me, my eyes widened and my heart started racing. I threw away my trash and stood up to go back to meet the guys. "Thanks for the heads up, Cass," I halfheartedly smiled at her. "But I can do this, whatever 'this' is. I won't let anything stop me from passing these tests. I know the trainer is supposed to be scary, but nothing is worse than what I'm already going through. Who is this trainer anyway?" I asked.

Cassie just smiled and gave me her famous wink, telling me she was keeping her mouth shut on this one. I guess I'd find out soon enough.

Cassie left to go on rounds and I went back into the training center. There, standing with James and Adam was the infamous Queen Elizabeth I. She no longer wore the enormously collared and ruffled corseted gowns with hooped skirts and petticoats or rice powder makeup, but there was no mistaking who she was. It was funny to see her in modern clothes, looking more like a trainer at a gym than British royalty. She wore no makeup and had her hair pulled into a tight bun at the nape of her neck. Large diamond stud earrings sparkled in her ears. They had to be at least a carat each. She was wearing a turquoise track suit with a back Lycra tank top underneath. Black Skeletoes running shoes were on her feet, and I tried hard not to giggle at the sight. Those shoes looked funny on a normal person, but on the Virgin Queen who actually attended Shakespeare's plays, they looked hysterical. I wandered over, debating in my head how to address her. Elizabeth? Your majesty? Hey, Liz? I glanced from James to Adam, hoping they would take the lead with introductions and end my internal debate.

"Lucy, may I introduce you to your trainer for the next several hours. This is Elizabeth," James said while Adam was trying hard to hold in a snicker. I knew he noticed her shoes too. I shot him a look telling him to knock it off before I started laughing and I made my face serious again before I smiled at her.

"It's a pleasure to meet you," I greeted her, careful not to use any name for fear of getting it wrong.

"Max practically begged me to come. I've come here on my day off, so you'd better be worth it. It is my understanding you wish to be trained as a Guide?" the Queen began and I nodded in agreement. "Don't think I'm going to go easy on you just because you're only doing it temporarily."

"No ma'am, I wouldn't dream of it."

"Then tell me child, why would you put yourself through this? I'm sure you've heard by now how rigorous the training can be," She looked at me with a stare that would make the strictest librarian cringe.

"Because I'd do anything for my sister. No matter how tough it is on me," I explained. "Now, where do we begin?" I wouldn't let her see my fear. I wouldn't cringe even though my heart was pounding out of nervousness.

"Eager," the Queen remarked, dragging the first word out so she almost purred. "Either I should be impressed or she's dimwitted. Time will tell." She nodded slightly at me before turning to James. "How much does she know? How much prep work has she had?"

"She's had hand to hand combat training, weapons training, and currently holds the record on the timed obstacle course," Pride was evident in his face. "She has been briefed on our history, but will need work in transferring realms and shielding."

"And I only have twelve hours to work with her?" she scoffed. "Well we have no time to waste!" Adam apparently took that as his queue to leave and headed for the door in a jog. He must have realized that he couldn't contain his laughter if he stayed.

"Coward!" I muttered under my breath as I waved goodbye.

"What was that?" the Queen asked.

"Oh, um, nothing. Just saying goodbye," I stammered out. The last thing I wanted was the Queen thinking I'd been referring to her instead of Adam.

"Fine then, Lucy, let's get started. We'll start with Shielding. This is a technique that Guide's often use that makes their charge appear invisible to any potential threats. Remember that once a person dies, humans can't see their souls but Vampires, Werewolves, and the Fae can. You'll need to be able to hide them from view so they can't be taken. This drains a lot of power, so only do it if a threat has presented itself."

"How do I create and use a Shield?" I asked, relieved that some of my initial fear had gone away, replaced with the excitement of learning something new.

"I'm going to demonstrate first and we'll use my assistant as the person whom you should be shielding." She pressed on her bracelet and leaned in to talk in to it, reminding me of a CIA or Secret Service agent. "Amelia, I need you in the training center now please." I looked over at James and his eyes widened and face blushed but grew a bright smile. Whoever the assistant was, he seemed to like her. Elizabeth turned back to me and continued talking. "Amelia is my number two and one of the best Guides we have. Between the two of us you might be able to learn enough to not be completely incompetent."

"Um, thanks. I guess," I replied. We only had to wait a minute before the training room doors burst open, and a tall, slender woman with short brown curly hair and a small gap in her two front teeth strode in with all the confidence of a Parisian runway model. She looked familiar, but I couldn't place her. James got to his feet quickly and began smoothing back his hair. I smiled, enjoying seeing him slightly rattled for once. Amelia stopped just in front of the Queen and stood almost at attention.

"How can I help you today, Boss?" she asked. I half expected her to salute!

"Amelia, this is Lucy, one of our newest recruits. She has been granted permission to Guide an eleven year old girl, and we only have twelve hours to prepare her. While James here boasts of her talents, I am not convinced of them myself. I'm going to need you to help us role-play by acting as her charge while we do some initial Guide training, and then we'll move on to you taking a stab at her while I observe her weaknesses, of which I'm sure there'll be plenty."

"Hey!" I protested, offended that she made assumptions about me before even seeing what I could do. Neither Elizabeth nor Amelia responded, but both rolled their eyes and conferred with each other for a few minutes. I sidled next to James and crossed my arms over my chest.

"That was a little rude, even for a Queen," I huffed. James didn't respond so I poked him in the ribs, but he was not paying attention to me at all. He was totally focused on

Amelia. He tucked in his shirt and wiped his face with his sleeve. I nudged him gently with my shoulder, "Amelia huh?" I teased. "Do you have a little crush?"

He turned the shade of ripe beets and shushed me. Here was an honored Army Sergeant Major, blushing like a schoolboy. I couldn't let him off the hook that easily so I continued teasing him a bit, "She's very pretty— familiar for some reason. You should ask her out. Invite her to dinner sometime." I had never seen this side of him, and it was amusing to say the least.

"I can't ask Amelia Earhart to dinner! Are you crazy? She'd never be interested in me. And keep your voice down! I don't want her hearing you," James hissed at me.

"*The* Amelia Earhart? Are you kidding me? Wow. I can't believe I'm being trained by two of the greatest women in history. Do you have any idea what each of them did to help push the women's movement forward to where it is today? Did you know that Amelia refused to accept her husband's name after they got married and told reporters when they'd refer to her by her married name that they were equal breadwinners and said maybe they should refer to him as Mr. Earhart? And that she was one of the first people to start an all-woman owned and operated business? Did you know that Elizabeth refused to marry because she knew a woman could do just as good of a job running a country as a man?" I was star struck. I could have talked for hours about them, but I wasn't given the chance when Elizabeth came back towards us.

"Let's get started, shall we? Shielding is a technique that allows you to hide either yourself or another person. It's to be used as a way to reposition for attack, reload your weapon, or simply hide." The Queen disparaged me for a moment before she continued with a sneer, "I'm sure you'll choose the hiding."

I was about to give her a piece of my mind when I saw James sternly looking my way, letting me know I was to keep my mouth shut. I bit my tongue literally to keep from retorting and waited for her to continue.

"I'm going to ask James to help out while I demonstrate how to effectively put up a shield around Amelia while James tries to attack her. Watch what I do so you can *attempt* to replicate it yourself," she explained, emphasizing attempt.

I watched as James headed to the other side of the room and used his bracelet to draw two small daggers, one in each hand. Amelia stood behind Elizabeth, who appeared bored and was playing with her nails. James ran at full force towards the women, only to stop about ten feet away and veer to the left before charging them again. He was trying to surprise them, but Elizabeth was ready. With a simple wave of her hand a bubble went around Amelia, and she was no longer visible.

James still went after the spot where she'd last been standing, but bounced off as he hit the invisible barrier and flew backwards, landing hard into the bleachers. He didn't stay down for long and got right back up, shaking his head a little as he twisted the daggers in his hands and looked back at Elizabeth. He charged again, this time using a zig-zag pattern that even with my enhanced sight, I could barely see as he moved rapidly towards his target. He must have realized that Amelia wouldn't be in the same spot and jumped high into the air, landing behind Elizabeth and trying to stab her from behind. I gasped thinking he would hurt the Queen, but she easily dodged his attack and sent him flying backwards again with a hard shove. I couldn't believe how this petite royal could throw around buff and brawny James like it was nothing more than tossing socks into the hamper.

James got up again, and I wondered if his third attempt would be the charm. He didn't charge right away, but began gazing around the room intensely. I looked around too trying to figure out what he was searching for. He seemed to have found it because he smirked slightly out of the side of his mouth. He threw one of his daggers directly at me and threw the other at Elizabeth and had conjured up two more before I could blink. I closed my eyes, screamed and ducked as the blade came towards me, but never heard it land. I opened one of my eyes while still keeping my hands covering my head and noticed Amelia was sitting directly in front of me. She had apparently caught the dagger and was smiling at James.

"Well played James," Amelia complimented. "How did you know where I was?"

"I knew you'd be in the place I'd least likely throw my dagger. And I was right."

"Yes, but you didn't hit me now did you. I caught your dagger."

"True, but if you had been and eleven year old girl, you wouldn't have. So I win," He stated as he puffed up his chest in accomplishment.

"No, you didn't win. I dropped the shield in order to allow myself to catch it. If I hadn't, it would have bounced off of me like you did the last two times," Amelia retorted, clearly amused and almost flirtatious.

"Enough you two," Elizabeth commanded. "James, your attempts were juvenile at best, and I expect better from you. Amelia, stop flirting. We have work to do."

At that, James blushed again, and I noticed the same rose hue on Amelia's face before she turned it away from my view. Oh, I liked this new twist. I couldn't wait to talk to Cassie about it later! My thoughts were quickly squelched by the Queen continuing, "Lucy, were you able to grasp any of the techniques we used in our demonstration?"

I shook my head no, but didn't want her to think that I was a complete idiot so I quickly added, "I saw that the shield is not able to be penetrated from direct hits or above either by person or weapon. I also noticed that you didn't have to be in direct contact with it in order to keep it up, but I'm not quite sure how you conjured it in the first place. I saw your hand sweep over her, but that's all I noticed."

"Hmm, maybe you're not as useless as I thought," she replied and my smile disappeared before she continued. "Creating a shield is simple enough, but it requires a lot of sustained energy to maintain it. Even one half second of not focusing can bring it down and expose your charge. That's the most important thing, never lose focus! I'm going to show you how to create a shield around James, then Amelia and I will attempt to distract you and get you to drop it."

She showed me how to create one, and I was able to do so. It was weird, when someone created the shield, the person in it wasn't invisible to them, but they appeared to be under water, having a liquidy appearance. While I was able to make the shield without problems, I couldn't seem to keep it up for more than a few seconds. It felt like it was draining all of my energy out of me and no matter how hard I focused, it would slip away. James continued to encourage me, but Elizabeth was like a pit bull, looking for any sign of weakness to attack.

"This is pathetic! You're going to kill your sister and yourself for the second time. Are you even trying? This is a waste of my time!" she screamed at me after my tenth slip up. I tried not to let it get to me, but it was hard to ignore. What if I couldn't protect Jessica?

"You need to TRY HARDER!" she berated as I focused all of my energy on keeping the shield around James. "Are you incompetent? Were you dropped on your head as a child and have brain damage? Why can't you focus?"

We'd been at it for two hours and I'd made almost no progress on keeping my shield up. I only had a few more hours before my time was up with them and if I couldn't master this by then, I couldn't guide Jessica. We started over, having Amelia try to distract me while I tried to put my shield around James. I ground my teeth together and refused to let the Shield slip. I was sweating profusely and felt the salty drop fall into my eye and cause it to sting. I closed my eyes and wiped it away quickly, but that's all it took to lose the Shield again.

"Damn it!" I screamed out in frustration. I immediately put the shield back up and called out, "Again!" Amelia didn't use verbal attacks to distract me like Elizabeth did, but instead attacked me physically. She would run into me and knock me down or pour a cup of cold water over my head. Once, she even bit me in the leg. I was getting better at being able to keep the shield up after the first attack, but if there were multiple attacks, like when Amelia spit in my face and Elizabeth yelled at the same time, I'd lose it instantly. I knew they were only trying to give me scenarios that I might actually face against a vampire or werewolf, but it didn't make it any easier. I put the shield down and staggered away with my hands on my hips and bent over at the waist trying to catch my breath. "I need five minutes," I announced and headed into the locker room. Standing at the sink, I splashed cold water on my face repeatedly and slurped some of it up, feeling parched. I grabbed a towel from the counter and dried my face. When I lowered it, James was sitting on the center bench between the lockers just staring at me, hands clasped.

"I know this is hard Lucy. It takes most Patroni months to get to the level you were able to today. You're doing a great job, honestly. Don't beat yourself up," he said, calming me down slightly.

"I need to be able to do this James. I can't fail."

"When you go back out there, I want you to try this. I want you to think of the shield as bullet proof glass. It will be less liquidy and will hold stronger, using less energy from you."

"You can see the shield?" I asked. The thought had never occurred to me.

"Yes, I can because I'm inside of it. But they can't which is why they're not able to explain what you need to do better. Your shield needs to be impenetrable, so make it so! It will be easier for you to focus on keeping it up if you're not worrying about it popping or bursting open."

"Thank you, James! That's excellent advice!" I smiled at him. "Let's go kick some royal butt, shall we?" He smiled back at me and we walked back into the training room. Elizabeth and Amelia were waiting for me, having just finished taking drinks from their sports bottles. They hadn't even broken a sweat! "All right ladies, let's try this again."

"You think you've got it this time?" Elizabeth taunted.

"I'm ready for you," I boasted, my confidence high after talking to James.

"Well, I'm going to warn you now that we've got a secret weapon," Amelia said with a sly grin on her face.

I didn't let her shake me. I took James's advice and put the shield up, making it like bullet proof glass instead of a liquid bubble. It seemed so simple; I wondered why I hadn't thought of it before. They started in on me, Amelia ramming me from the side, and Elizabeth screaming how my parents must be so disappointed in me, but I didn't let it faze me. I spun out of Amelia's attack and kept my focus on James. They kept their attack going, but after twenty minutes they still hadn't gotten me to drop it. I was smiling now, finding it easier to maintain focus with this new technique and it wasn't using as much energy. I continued to dodge and roll out of Amelia's physical attacks and now barely heard Elizabeth in the background. After being knocked down once again, Amelia got up and gave a quick nod to Elizabeth. I knew they'd be releasing their secret weapon soon so I doubled my focus on James. Suddenly, the side door opened and Max sauntered through, wearing only swimming trunks and flip flops. His shirtless chest in all of its beautiful glory was all I saw walking towards me. The muscles flexed and rippled as he walked, and I'm pretty sure I started drooling a little. This was so not fair. How was I supposed to concentrate with him looking more sinful than my favorite dessert? He smiled that award-winning smile. The dimple in his cheek made an appearance, and I lost my focus. James popped back into view for everyone to see and Amelia seized the opportunity. She threw her weapon (this time she used a nine inch knife) directly at James. Luckily he caught it. Elizabeth smirked in victory, and I was defeated. It was hard to be too sad with Max standing there half naked. I had to fight to keep my hands at my sides and not rub his chest.

"Hey, Lucy," Max greeted me with a smile that made my knees buckle before turning to the others, "Elizabeth, you wanted to see me? You know I was working on arrangements for Lucy's mission, so why am I here and why did you tell me to wear my swim trunks?"

I turned to stare daggers at Elizabeth who had a smirk on her face I was itching to smack off. I couldn't believe she manipulated Max into coming down here just to mess with me! That was playing dirty, and even worse, she knew I wouldn't call her out on it in front of Max! At least Max wasn't in on the plan and wasn't trying to help her.

"Yes, Max. Thank you for coming so promptly. We're going to need you for the next part of our training for Lucy. Plus I figured since you'd worked so hard on getting me here to train her, you'd like to see her utter lack of success or even progress. For the time being, you can watch on the sidelines," Elizabeth smirked.

"No, that's not necessary. We have several hours still here, Max. Feel free to go back to whatever you were doing before Elizabeth so rudely pulled you away," I retorted. I knew she was trying to keep him there to distract me and I didn't want to allow him to be used in that way.

"Actually, I finished all of my errands and finished my rounds for the day. I have plenty of free time now and I'd love to help you with your training anyway I can," Max said. Of all the dumb luck! I finally get him shirtless and asking to spend time with me and it's at the worst possible time! I couldn't say no to that offer, so I smiled and thanked him before watching him trot off to the bleachers to observe me in action.

Eleven

Elizabeth and Amelia wasted no time in returning to their assaults. I quickly formed a shield and James instantly became invisible to them. I turned my back to Max in order to prevent any more distractions. Amelia came at me full force, this time aiming her dagger at me. I dropped low to the ground and swept my foot out to catch her legs. She tumbled, but rolled out of it and slammed her elbow into my kidney. I winced from the pain, but didn't drop the shield. She tried again with the knife, barely missing my arm as I rolled away and shot to my feet. Max cheered me on in the background and pride swelled inside me. Elizabeth saw the happiness and pride in my face and began her own assaults.

"So, Lucy, think you can you protect your charge and your boyfriend?" she taunted. "You may have to choose, so who's it going to be? What if you can only save one?" At that moment, I realized what she had planned. She pulled out a sword and went for Max while Amelia caught my foolish glances towards James that gave away his location. She began heading right for him. What was I supposed to do? There were two threats and only one of me. Could I expand the shield so it covered both of them? No, they were too far apart. I couldn't risk exposing James, but I couldn't let Max get hurt either. I ran towards Max, putting myself directly in front of him as he stood up from the bench where he was watching. I could see the confusion on Max's face as he realized he was now a part of the game and no longer a spectator who could sit passively by.

I could see out of the corner of my eye that James had moved and Amelia was no longer a threat to him, but now both women were coming directly for me and Max, weapons drawn. Our demise seemed imminent. I felt Max against my back, but he was trapped by the bleachers and unable to run. I had mere seconds to do something before it was game over, and I'd lose both Max and my sister. I had no idea what to do; I hadn't been trained for this. I quickly ran through options in my head, but they were all flawed. Time was up, so I said a silent prayer and went for the Hail Mary. Swiping my arm in a downward motion, I made a second shield that encompassed both myself and Max. I glanced back at James and was relieved to find his shield still intact. Amelia and Elizabeth both stopped in their tracks and looked baffled by what I'd just done. I felt two large hands on each of my biceps and Max leaned down to speak to me.

"I can't believe it!" he whispered in my ear, his breath tickling the hairs on my neck. "This is unbelievable!" His hands left my arms and he wrapped me in a hug, lifting me up so high I was wiggling my toes in the air. He spun me around in his excitement, and I had trouble not dropping the shields I'd created.

"Max, you need to put me down. I'm having trouble concentrating on the shields." It was taking everything I had to hold them up, and I was rapidly feeling the effects.

"Lucy, do you have any idea what you've done?" Max asked, astonished.

"Um, protected us?" I guessed. What else did he expect me to do? Did I do it wrong? Was creating two shields against the rules or something? I scanned the room for Elizabeth and Amelia and was surprised to see that their eyes were practically bugged out of their faces. "Okay, someone want to fill me in? Was I not supposed to do that?"

I dropped the shields, figuring this round was over and glad for it. I wasn't sure how much longer I could have kept them up. Creating two shields was exhausting, and I felt lightheaded after expending all that energy. I leaned against Max, suddenly unable to stay upright, and he gently helped me sit on the bench.

"I– I can't believe you were able to do that!" Elizabeth stammered. "In all my years I've never seen anyone without at least 100 years of training be able to create and hold two shields."

"You mean not everyone can create more than one shield?" I asked, watching each person slowly shake their heads as I fought the dizziness in mine. "Why was I able to do it?"

"The better question is *how* were you able to do it," Amelia answered.

"I don't know." I tried to think back to my actions. "I knew I couldn't let James's shield drop and I knew Max and I needed protection since you were coming at us with weapons, and we had nowhere to go. It was the only thing I could think to do," I shrugged.

"Simply amazing," Amelia murmured as James nodded in agreement. I wasn't sure what to make of this whole thing and turned to Max for support. He smiled and sat next to me, taking my hand and lacing our fingers together before speaking.

"Lucy, the amount of energy it takes to not only create but hold two shields is extreme. Think of it as having a AA battery power an entire New York City skyscraper. It's extremely draining and even with our heightened abilities, there are only a few of us who can do it. Most people have to practice for decades before they can create two, and then practice for a few more decades before they can hold them for any period of time. You were able to do both after a few hours of training. It's just not done," he explained and I felt awed by his words even as a fought to keep my eyes open. I was completely exhausted.

"I don't know what to say," I babbled. "Am I some sort of prodigy? A freak of nature? Was this a fluke? Does this mean I passed and can help my sister?" So many questions were flowing out of me no one knew which to answer first. Max placed his other hand on top of the one he was already holding, and I stopped talking.

"Let's start by seeing if you can do it again. Maybe it was a lucky first try or maybe you are truly amazingly gifted." He squeezed my hand at the second option letting me know he was betting on the latter. I let out a deep breath and attempted to stand. I was still lightheaded, so Max helped me by keeping his hand on my back to ensure I didn't fall over.

"Maybe we should give you a little more time to rest," he continued, taking charge of the situation. "You're obviously still drained from the first time and I don't think you're ready to give it a go again so quickly. James, will you get me her water bottle. Elizabeth, I'm assuming you're okay with waiting a little longer to try again? Shall we meet back here in an hour?"

"Yes, of course," Elizabeth agreed as Amelia nodded next to her. "Amelia, let's go get some recording equipment so we can capture her next attempt on video to analyze later."

The two of them trotted gaily out the doors, James followed behind them to see if he could "help" carry anything. I smiled knowing the real reason for his gentlemanly gesture was to spend a little more time with Amelia. I wasn't upset. It gave me a few alone minutes with Max. I turned to sit back down, still finding it difficult to see straight, but Max kept me upright.

"Let's find you somewhere more comfortable to rest," he suggested.

"Really, I'm fine here Max. Besides, I don't think I have the energy to make it back to the Commons or anything." Before I could continue my protests, he scooped me up and began carrying me. "Max, this isn't necessary. I can stay on these benches for a little while."

"I'm not taking you to the Commons or your room," he explained, "I'm taking you to the physical therapy room. There's a hot tub in there that'll help you relax, and the warm water should help you recover some of your energy. Water has natural healing powers." He continued carrying me to an area I hadn't seen before. It was much like the room my athletic trainers used in my old life. There were massage tables, ice baths, and two whirlpool tubs in the back. A sign indicating a sauna was off to the left and racks of fresh towels were set out on a nearby bar.

"Um, Max?" I don't have a swimsuit with me." I looked around nervously, trying to figure out what I should do. Max was already in his swim trunks, but I was wearing running shorts and a sports bra. And while that would probably suffice for relaxing in the hot tub, I wouldn't have any dry clothes to change into afterwards.

"Not a problem. There are several extras stocked in the closet over there. I'll leave you to change and be back in a minute to help you into the tub," Max explained before turning around and strolling out.

I lethargically made my way across the room to the closet in the back and opened the door. There were one and two piece swimsuits in a multitude of colors and sizes. I picked out a solid black one piece with a racerback and quickly put it on, not wanting to be half dressed when Max walked back in. I sat on the bench and scowled in the mirror before deciding to run my fingers through my knotted hair. I grabbed the hair tie off of my wrist and quickly tossed my hair into a loose twist just to keep it from getting soaked and hoped that the steam didn't make my hair frizz out too badly— although I knew it was inevitable with my thick, naturally wavy hair. What I wouldn't have given for a little Infusium 23.

Max knocked before coming back in and I didn't bother to get up. I was still too exhausted. He scooped me up again and carried me up the two stairs before stepping over the edge and sinking both of us into the warm, steamy water. I thought he would move me to his side or even across from him, but he held me on his lap, turning me so I was resting against his chest. I wasn't going to argue, and I was too tired to try even if I wanted to. I closed my eyes and stretched my legs out so my toes touched the other side of the tub as I listened to the sounds of the water bubbling. My muscles became less tense as I lay there. I wasn't sure if it was the water or being near Max that was helping me relax. He rubbed my shoulders gently, and I felt my body melting. Delightful shivers danced across my skin.

"Are you feeling better yet?" Max asked after several minutes. I mumbled something in the affirmative and kept my eyes closed, relaxing against him. I wondered for the hundredth time why I felt so comfortable being near him in this way, why it felt natural. If any other guy I wasn't dating had done this, my mind would be racing with questions about how I looked, what he was thinking or what should I say to fill the silence. With Max, the silence wasn't uncomfortable. It was tranquil. I didn't feel the need to chatter away about the weather, last night's episode of some TV show, or make small talk. I just knew I was happy when I was around him and that he was happy around me. Of course I still wondered why he kept his distance lately, but that was a question for another time.

After another twenty minutes or so in the hot tub, I felt my energy returning. I took a deep breath, allowing the steam to fill my lungs and unclog my head of the dizziness and nausea. I sat up slightly, stretching my hands towards my toes and enjoying the pull on my hamstrings. Max laughed as I tried to do the Warrior One pose in the hot tub, but I knew the yoga positions would help get me ready for the next few hours of training and help loosen up some of my stiff muscles.

"You're not going to try Sun Salutations in the tub too, are you?" he joked, splashing me a little with the water.

I jabbed him playfully in the arm and retorted, "Yep, right after you do the Bow position on the bottom of the tub!' I pictured him on his stomach, arching his back and grabbing his ankles under the water and laughed.

"Let's get out of the whirlpool and do some real yoga." He held out his arm to help me out of the tub.

"You do yoga?"

"Yes, as a matter of fact I do," he confirmed without any embarrassment.

I could count on one hand the number of guys who attended my yoga class at the gym, and most of them were coerced by their girlfriends.

"Yoga is a great meditation tool as well as a great way to keep toned", Max continued. "With our enhanced brain power, it can get a little overwhelming if we don't shut down and reboot every once in a while."

"Wow. I just never would have imagined. Okay, let's do this. But if you get stuck in Plow position, don't expect me to help you out of it!" Being bent like a pretzel your feet behind your head wasn't easy, though I wouldn't mind seeing his cute tush in the air.

Max wrapped a big fluffy towel around me, taking a second to give me a brief hug that made my heart flutter before taking off for the men's changing rooms. Wishing I had brought a change of clothes, I searched the closet where I found the swimsuit. Sure enough, there were several sets of tee shirts and shorts. I found an Under Armor tank top and a pair of shorts, changed quickly, and met him back in the training center.

When I got there, he was unrolling two yoga mats and connecting his iPod to the speakers. I stood on the mat next to him and let him call out different poses. My mind focused only on the poses and the sound of the music as I relished the stretch and pull of my muscles as I completed each pose. This was exactly what I needed to focus and prepare for another grueling few hours of training. As I positioned myself into Side Plank, balancing on one hand and foot as I reached for the sky, I spied Max from the corner of my eye and had to admit I was impressed by how many poses he had mastered. I decided to challenge him a bit and began calling out a few myself. I smiled, thinking about watching him try poses that his 6'5" frame would shriek at.

"Crane pose," I called out before lowering myself to all fours and placing my knees on my elbows. It took me months to master this pose without falling over, so I giggled and watched Max try it. To my surprise, he went right down in it and held it without wobbling once. Well I'll be damned, Max was a yoga guru. I wondered what else I didn't know about him? *Gee, I guess I'll have to force myself to spend more time with him to find out,* I thought wickedly.

We were completing Sun Salutations when James, Amelia, and Elizabeth came back in. They allowed us another minute to finish before turning off the iPod and urging us to get back to the training. I felt a hundred times better than when I'd last I saw them and I let my wicked thoughts continue. *I'll have to find a way to thank Max for making me feel better. Maybe some way to make him feel better...*

I turned my thoughts back to why we were here before my own musings made me blush. They had some recording equipment with them and began to set it up at the top of the bleachers. They placed three HD camcorders with attached microphones and additional lighting down at different angles around the room so it could take in the whole area. After they pressed the record button, I positioned myself in the middle of the court and waited for further instructions.

"Okay, Lucy," Elizabeth began. "I'm going to try to attack you from two different angles. I want you to try to put a shield around both James and Amelia. I'll have them stand near each other, so we can see if proximity matters." I nodded before hearing her whisper under her breath, "If you can even do it again. I'm sure it was a fluke."

Determined to prove her wrong, I focused all of my energy and created a shield around Amelia first, then tried to make one around James. He was only standing about ten feet from her, so I debated if I could just use one giant shield or if I should try to make two separate ones. In the end, I tried for two, thinking it was a better test of my skills. Amelia disappeared from view rather easily, but even after focusing for several minutes I was having trouble putting up a second one for James. I could see Elizabeth smirking off to the side and I redoubled my efforts, not wanting her to feel a victorious.

"Having trouble, Lucy?" the Queen smirked.

"I don't know what I'm doing differently from last time," I huffed, frustrated at myself.

"I have an idea," Max commented. "Last time, we were both under attack before you were able to pull out the second shield. Maybe there needs to be imminent danger for you to draw that much energy? Elizabeth, begin the attack and let's see if that helps."

Elizabeth pulled weapons out of her outfit that she'd previously conjured and stored away. I didn't realize a tracksuit could hold so many! She had guns, knives, a long sword, and I counted at least five daggers. Here was the Virgin Queen, packing more heat than the Sopranos! She backed up slightly, widening her attack area so I couldn't see who she'd go for first. I spread my arms out so I'd be ready and rolled slightly on the balls of my feet with nervous anticipation.

She picked up her gun, a Walther PPK in her right hand and had two Chinese throwing stars in her other. I knew the attack would come fast, and I prayed I'd be able to protect both of them. At once, she fired the gun towards Amelia, who was already shielded. Then, she threw the stars. To my surprise, she threw one at James and one to my far left at Max who was sitting on the sidelines. I was horrified to realize he was in harm's way without being prepared for it. I could feel my heart racing to prevent any damage. In the blink of an eye, I easily threw a second shield at James and ran towards Max. The second star was travelling too fast, and I wouldn't get there in time to block him. It was now only inches from him and even if he ducked it would have hit him. I screamed out and flung my arm at Max, encapsulating him in a third shield a quarter of a second before the star would have sliced through him and I fell to the ground. The star pinged off of it and rolled harmlessly away. I squeezed my eyes shut in relief and let out the breath I'd been holding.

Seeing that no one was hurt I got to my feet and brushed off my knees. As immortals, James and Max would have been fine, but it wouldn't have been pretty and I couldn't stand the thought of them being in pain because I'd failed to protect them.

"You bitch!" I screamed out. "What were you thinking? Max wasn't supposed to be a target! You could have really hurt him!"

"I was testing your abilities, and it's a good thing I did," she stated calmly, a genuine smile spreading across her face. "Do you have any idea how remarkable your abilities are or how rare what you accomplished is? Creating two shields takes decades to do, and you created three on your first day. Un-fucking-believable. Do you know I wasn't able to create three for almost two hundred years?"

My jaw dropped and Max ran over, enveloping me in a hug and spinning me around. James too was patting me on the back and offering congratulations. I was so worried about Max getting hurt I didn't even stop to think about how I was able to protect him. I was still in disbelief and couldn't believe what I had done. If what she was telling me was true, then I had passed! I passed the test no one thought I could!

I'd be able to Guide Jessica! Excitement welled in me, and I squeezed Max tightly. He kissed the top of my head and I felt I might burst from happiness.

"We need to continue to see what you can do," Amelia interjected, obviously hesitant to ruin my happy moment. "We need to test you to see your range of abilities. We're going to need more help. I'll be back momentarily. I'm going to call the rest of your team in." She trotted off towards the door, her hand already pressing her bracelet to call them. I was still standing next to Max with his arm around me, but suddenly I felt ready to pass out. My knees became weak and lightheadedness overtook me once more. I put my arms tightly around Max's waist to keep from falling over. He glanced at me and immediately helped me sit down.

"We're going to need to wait for a bit, Elizabeth. The energy has been drained out of her and she'll need to rest before doing anything else, "he pointed out, not as a request but as a demand.

I tried to protest, knowing that we had precious little time to waste, but my eyes were so heavy I was having trouble just keeping them open, let alone remaining upright for practice. I nodded and closed my eyes, planning to just to rest them for a few moments until everyone arrived.

When I opened my eyes, I was laying on a couch in one of the offices with one of Max's sweatshirts balled up underneath my head for a pillow. I took a deep breath, relishing the scent of him on the shirt as I did so. I wondered if he'd notice if I kept it. I smiled at the thought of waking up every day to his woodsy, musky scent and thought of the yummy daydreams I could have imagining him next to me in bed. With an even broader smile plastered on my face, I stretched and stood up, peering around to see if anyone was nearby. I didn't see anyone, so I proceeded out of the office and down the small hallway towards the main training area where I'd been all day.

I hoped I hadn't been asleep for long and still had enough time to train before Marco called us with the order to go. I had set an alarm on my bracelet to keep track of how much time I had left and pulled it out now to check. I still had four hours before my training time was up with Elizabeth and then another twenty four hours before it was time to go. I sighed, glad I hadn't wasted too much time.

When I made it to the training room, I saw that the rest of my team were gathered and being briefed by Elizabeth. Max and James were off to the side, since they already knew what was going on. They were deep in conversation. I stepped into the room and everyone turned when they heard me enter. Max rushed to my side, almost protectively, and Cassie skipped over, hugging me and congratulating me on the accomplishments. Adam, as usual, held back, but offered a nod and a smile to let me know he was proud of me. I let go of Cassie and turned to face everyone. Max still stood protectively at my side and took my hand in his. Butterflies did somersaults in my stomach, and I swallowed them down before addressing the group.

"I'm so sorry I passed out like that. I couldn't seem to keep my eyes open. Creating multiple shields is extremely tiring." Everyone nodded in agreement so I continued, "How do I keep from passing out while on assignment?" I asked.

"Time and practice," Elizabeth said, no longer as hostile now that I passed her tests. "It won't come overnight, which is why I worry still about your upcoming assignment. I have no doubts you'll be able to protect your sister if there is an attack, but for how long? What if the attack was drawn out or carried out by multiple assailants? How long before you pass out and leave her vulnerable?"

"I have the same worries, but luckily, I won't be there by myself. Max will be with me," I responded, squeezing his hand as I said it.

"Yes and between the two of us, nothing will happen to Jessica," Max vowed. "But I won't allow you to do what you're thinking, Elizabeth. She's not some lab rat you can poke and prod to see if she says 'ow'. I won't let you do this." I squinted at him having no idea what he was talking about.

"We need to know what she's capable of. And who are you to tell me no? I outrank you Max! You can't keep your little girlfriend all to yourself," Elizabeth snarled back. I hadn't been afraid of her before, but with the death glare she gave Max, I found myself clinging to him as he pushed me behind him to keep me out of reach. Max didn't answer her, but returned her stare. With his tall, muscular frame towering over the petite woman ready to attack, I couldn't believe she wasn't backing down.

"What is she talking about?" I asked my team, but didn't get an answer.

"You're right, you do outrank Max," James interceded, stepping between Max and Elizabeth before either of them could move. "But you don't outrank me. *I'm* telling you no."

Elizabeth was fuming, and I was glad I was behind both Max and James. That woman scared the pants off of me. Amelia took a step forward and put her arms out in an attempt to stave off both parties. "I think we've gotten ahead of ourselves. Let's all just all take a step back. Max, we don't want to experiment on her, we just want to put her through a few physical tests to see what she's capable of. I'm sure she'll be okay with it. If it was me, I'd want to know how far my abilities reached. We're not looking to make a freak show out of her, right Elizabeth?" she said, staring at the Queen to get her to nod in agreement.

"If someone could just fill me in on what you all are talking about, then maybe someone can ask my opinion, since whatever you're talking about obviously involves me!" I added, angry to have people talking about me as if I wasn't here.

Max turned to me, still keeping me far away from Elizabeth. "They want to experiment on you and put you through painful tests to see how useful you'll be to them," he explained.

"You want to do *what*?" I asked incredulously. "Is this true, Elizabeth?"

"It's not that bad," she protested. "We just want to see how far your abilities reach. And the only way to do that is to test them. It may be painful, but that pain is only temporary."

"Max is right Elizabeth. I'm not some lab rat. I don't want to be experimented on. But none of this is important now. We need to focus on getting me ready to help Jessica. I only have a few hours left with you, and we haven't even started working on transferring between realms. So we're tabling this discussion. Okay?"

Elizabeth and Max kept their stare-down going, neither wanting to be the first to back down. "I said, *okay*?" I repeated more firmly. Max sighed and nodded. He wasn't happy to end things, but he did as I requested. Elizabeth smiled broadly, thinking she'd won her little contest with Max. The look she gave Max made me angry, and I couldn't hold back any longer. "Oh knock it off, Elizabeth! You didn't win the little staring contest. Max chose to be the bigger person and the grown up so move on. Stop acting like a child!"

She didn't like being called out and quickly turned on her heel, humphing as she went. Amelia caught her before she left entirely, and I knew she was convincing her to stay and help train me. Elizabeth's pride was hurt and it wouldn't be easy to convince her. After several tense minutes, her shoulders slumped down in defeat and Amelia turned and smiled towards us, giving me a thumbs-up. While we may have convinced her to continue to train me, I knew she'd be more brutal than before.

Two hours later, I was exhausted to the point I could barely stand. I had multiple cuts and scrapes that were trying to heal, and I was soaking wet from sweat. I was right, Elizabeth made her previous training look like child's play compared to what she dished out now. But no matter how hard she made it, in the end I was able to make and hold multiple shields. I could make them from great distances, if the person inside was moving, or even if I was being attacked by more than one person. I was ready!

"All right Lucy, I think you're ready for realm changing training," James announced. I plopped down on my butt, not having the energy to walk the five steps to a seat and groaned. I closed my eyes and took a few deep breaths, trying to summon any energy I had to the surface so I could continue. No matter how hard I tried, I just didn't have anything left. My tank was empty. James agreed to give me some time to rest before beginning again. I mumbled my appreciation and lay down directly on the floor, unable and unwilling to move. Cassie knelt down next to me and tried to help me up.

"You can't sleep here, Luc! This floor is filthy! Let's move you to the couch again." She tried, but now that I was down and my eyes were closed, I couldn't even muster the thoughts to tell her no. She let go of my arm and stood up. I was just drifting off when I heard her talking to Max in hushed tones.

"You gonna take her?" Cassie asked Max.

"Yes, but I think I'll take her back to her own bed. She'll get better rest that way."

"So I assume that's where you'll be if we need you?" Cassie teased.

"You know there's nowhere else I'd rather be Cass."

"And you still haven't told her why?"

"We've been over this. It's not the right time. I don't want her to feel pressured when there's so much going on. I'm waiting until things calm down. She has to have time to understand and not freak out."

"Are you kidding? No matter when you tell her she's still going to freak out! How could she not?"

I couldn't focus on their words any longer and drifted away, wondering if they'd actually said it or if I was already dreaming.

Twelve

"Will you keep your voice down? You're going to wake her up!" Max whispered in harsh tones. "I'm trying to give her as much rest as possible so she's prepared for the next few hours."

"Sorry man, but they just scored! It's 24-0 State, so I got a little excited. What else am I supposed to do, sit and stare at her longingly as she sleeps like you?" Adam protested from the living room. My eyes fluttered open and I blinked a few times to try to make them focus. I was in my bedroom. Cassie and Max were there, and I could hear Adam and James in the other room cheering for a college football game. Cassie was painting her nails at my vanity and Max was sitting on the bed pretending to go through paperwork, but really he was only watching me. That made me smile as I sat up and stretched. I didn't have time to lay back and relax. This deadline Marco gave me was starting to make me crazy!

"Hey, guys," I addressed them as James and Adam strolled in. "I'm sorry I keep passing out on you all."

"Totally understandable," Cassie assured me as she put the final coat on her nails and began to wave her hands rapidly around to dry them.

"I know, but I still feel bad. It keeps happening and it's the worst possible time. I have so much to do; a nap doesn't really fit into my schedule."

"You're making more progress than anyone ever expected," James chimed in. "It's absolutely amazing what you've been able to accomplish in just a few hours. The whole community is abuzz with the news, and Adam actually tried to sell tickets to watch you practice!"

I looked at Adam as his face blushed slightly and he stared down at his feet. "There were several takers too! I wouldn't have had to do rounds for a month if James hadn't of stopped me." He chuckled before adding, "you're not mad are you Lucy?"

I thought about making him squirm for a while longer, but his sweet smile wore me down. "Of course not. I just hope you'd share some of that time off with me!"

"Deal!" he agreed quickly and we shook on it while everyone else erupted in giggles.

"All right, time to get serious," James said, taking charge as usual and bringing us back to business. "Lucy, you have about an hour and a half with Elizabeth still and since you've pretty much mastered shields, I think it's time to start training on changing realms."

"But I've already done it once. Sure it feels weird and takes some getting used to, but why does it involve training?" I asked.

"It's a little more complicated than it looks," Max answered for James. "The last time you did it, you were holding my hand so I took the brunt of the force. When you're changing realms with a minor, you're going to need to make sure they feel as comfortable as possible and that will mean you take control of several functions at once while feeling that intense pressure times ten."

"Oh, wow. I didn't realize how involved it was," I said, worried. "So how do I train for something like that?"

"We'll explain outside. Let's get going." James nodded and Cassie and Adam stood up and left the room. Max stood, but didn't go any further, obviously waiting for me. I brushed the covers aside and climbed out of bed. I realized I was still wearing the same clothes and I really wanted to change since I'd been sweating in them so much.

"Can I get a few minutes to freshen up and change guys?"

"Oh, sure. We'll be waiting just outside," Max reassured me before he and James proceeded out of the Dwelling and quietly shut the door behind them. I went into my adjoining bathroom and ran a warm washcloth over my face and arms before patting them dry with a fluffy towel. I stripped off my sweat soaked clothes and went back to my wardrobe, searching for attire appropriate for changing realms. Having no idea about what I'd need, I decided on a pair of comfortable jeans with holes in the knees, and a cute tee shirt that I always loved with a sarcastic saying on the front. I laced up my sneakers and opened the door looking for the guys. They were flipping through stations one right after another, obviously impatient, in the living room.

"Sorry it took me so long," I apologized. "I'm ready. Where to next?"

"We're going to the meadow where the Realm doors are. That area has the most realm doors available and there's lot of room to practice," James informed me.

Elizabeth was already waiting, but Amelia wasn't with her. I surveyed the group and waited for further instructions. Not surprisingly, James took the lead in explaining how this next phase was going to work.

"We're going to start by having you change realms by yourself. This will give you an idea of the force you'll feel once you take charge of a transfer."

"But what if I don't do it correctly? There'll be no one there to help me and I don't want to get stuck between two places!" Knowing me, I'd just float around for the next century waiting for someone to find me.

"Not possible. We're giving you a practice door to start with. The door will simply lead you out, and bring you right back in over here," Elizabeth noted, pointing out a door just to her left.

"And you're sure I won't get stuck?" I questioned, still not comfortable with the idea of going by myself.

"Well let me just put it to you this way, we've been using this for several centuries and we haven't lost anyone yet."

"There's always a first time," I muttered, knowing I was probably being irrational but unable to stop the words.

Max placed his hand in mine and gave it a gentle tug. "You can do this Lucy. Piece of cake!" he reassured me.

I steeled myself and went to stand next to the door. It helped knowing Max believed in me. Somehow it gave me confidence I knew wasn't really mine. I took a deep breath and placed my hand on the door handle. I glanced back at Max once more, needing to see him before taking this leap and his smile gave me what I needed. I turned it and stepped inside.

I instantly wanted to scream from the intensity of it, but couldn't force my mouth to open to let the sound out. I felt like my intestines were being knotted up like laces on tennis shoes and my bones seemed to bend with the pressure. I prayed every bone in my body wouldn't snap and even if they didn't, I would certainly need to visit to the chiropractor after this. I kept my eyes clenched shut for fear that my eyeballs would burst out of their sockets. Before I could even think about my destination, I came rolling out onto the grass with everyone huddled around me. I didn't try to get up, but just laid there in a ball with my eyes clenched for a few seconds. When I felt rough, calloused hands smoothly rub my back I knew Max was there. I wanted to turn to him, knowing the sight would calm me down, but I couldn't move a single muscle in my body. For a second, it was like I was completely paralyzed.

I tried to take a deep, calming breath, which was a wrong decision. As soon as I did, I felt the instantaneous need to vomit. I quickly pushed myself off the ground and ran to the tree line nearby to unload the contents of my stomach. Cassie quickly came over and gave me a bottle of water so I could rinse my mouth out. After several minutes, I stood up and headed back to the group. Max leaned forward, and I knew he was considering joining me, but since Cassie was already there, he stayed put. That saddened me because I knew feeling his heat and presence next to me would work faster than the Tums Cassie was trying to make me chew. I swallowed them anyway and drank a little more water. I was beginning to feel better, but dreading having to go through that all over again soon.

"What the hell was that?" I stuttered.

"That was the Bunny Hill of realm changes," The Queen scoffed. "If you can't handle that, you'll never be ready for the Black Diamond run that's coming."

I turned to Max and James for confirmation that what she was saying was true and wanted to cry when they nodded reluctantly in agreement. "Shit," I muttered, knowing I would need to figure out a way to master this or all of the training I'd put myself through for the last 40 plus hours would be worthless. "So how do I do this? Just keep going in and out until it doesn't affect me anymore? Why doesn't transferring realms affect you guys in the same way?" I focused on Max, because he'd seemed perfectly fine the last time we did it together. He moved to my side, placed his hands on my biceps and rubbed my arms gently as he answered me.

"It takes some getting used to," he started, but I snorted at his blasé reply so he continued trying to explain. "Your body just has to adjust to the changes you're putting it through. It's not an easy thing. Spirits have no body until they get here and are given solid form again, but we don't have that luxury when we're transferring realms. I know it feels like the most unnatural thing ever, and it can be painful at first, but it does get easier. This is where doing yoga helps. Try to bend your body with it rather than fight against it. Drink some more water and try it again," he urged.

I took another few sips, trying not to chug it so I didn't make myself sick again. I stretched my arms over my head and behind my back, hoping being loose and limber would ease the strain and marched up to the door. I stepped inside again and felt the same strains. I gritted my teeth and moved my body in rhythm with the force rather than fighting against it. It seemed to help. I didn't feel like dying from the agony, instead just felt like crying. I figured it was a step up. I kept my eyes shut because I still didn't trust my eyeballs to stay in their sockets. After a moment, it was over, and I was lying on the grass again surrounded by my team. Cassie was quick to hand me my bottle of water and tried to smooth my hair out of my face with a clip. It was now plastered to my face from sweating so much. I couldn't speak for a few seconds while I tried to catch my breath and keep my stomach from upchucking the water I had so carefully sipped.

Cassie, knowing I needed a break from the stress whispered in my ear, "You know, Lucy, you're making it hard for me to continue preaching my motto on girls and sweating."

I cocked my head to one side and raised my eyebrow in curiosity. Who has a motto on sweat? She read the skepticism on my face and explained. "It's quite simple really. The fact of the matter is girls don't sweat, they glisten. Sweating is a filthy sight and best left to boys. We girls are simply too pretty to allow ourselves to sweat. Therefore, instead of sweating buckets and becoming stinky, we glisten. It's much more pleasant."

I couldn't help but laugh and smile. Her attempt at vanquishing my stress worked. I stood up and brushed the grass off me.

"Well, you're not throwing up," James noted, "I take it you had an easier time of it on your second attempt?"

I nodded briefly. "I didn't want to die this time. So that's progress. I just don't know how I'm going to take this much pressure and the pressure of another person," I sighed. The clock continued to wind down and my progress was not coming swiftly enough. My anxiety built with every minute that passed.

"Well, remember," Max began, "I'll be there too. We'll each take a portion of it. But I can't take both yours and hers. You'll need to be able to handle this and a little more. Plus, we'll be traveling further than the practice door is taking you so you'll have to build your endurance."

I groaned at this realization and took a final swig of water, ready to try again, and hoping the third time would be the charm. "Okay, let's do this," I stated, hoping the bravado in my voice would convince my body to cooperate. I stood next to the door with my hand on the knob when I felt someone tapping my shoulder. I paused and turned around. I was surprised to see that it was Elizabeth standing behind me.

"Lucy, as much as I doubted your ability to be even remotely competent at the beginning of all of this, I applaud your progress. And as much as I hate to admit it, you're one of the best I've seen in centuries. While I still believe that you'll fail miserably at this task because you keep letting your emotions get in the way, I feel that I should give you another pointer."

I found her backhanded compliment amusing. Only she could tell you something positive while slapping you in the face so well. I held back my smile by biting the insides of my cheeks while I urged her to continue. Seeing Adam in my peripheral vision quickly turn around and take a few steps back, I knew he was fighting back laughter too. Even the corner of James's eyes twitched at her words. I kept my face forward for fear that seeing my friends reactions would be a fatal error.

Elizabeth didn't seem to notice any of this and continued, "Holding your breath makes it worse. I know you feel that your lungs are about to burst, but you can't hold that breath in. It only puts more pressure on the rest of your body.

Instead, just gradually let out a breath as if you would if you were holding your breath underwater for an extended period of time."

I thought about what she had said and could have smacked myself. Of course! It was one of the first things you learn in swim classes. You need to let some of the air out in order to stay underwater longer. I felt stupid I didn't think of it earlier. I smiled widely and thanked her. Then, I headed back to the door, turned the handle and let myself through once more.

As intense as the pressure was, when I let out a few air bubbles it didn't seem impossible. I even pried one of my eyes open slightly just to see if I could. I expected to see darkness surrounding me, but instead I could see bright shades of yellow, orange and red swirling around slightly. It was like walking into a sunset and it was one of the most beautiful things I'd ever seen. This must be the "bright light" people talk about seeing after they die. I opened my other eye to take it all in, awed by the beauty surrounding me and felt my heart lift in joy. I was doing it! I was handling the pressure and even enjoying the journey this time. I tried not to close my eyes for fear of missing even a microsecond of this, but the pressure forced me to blink. Before I could open my eyes again, I found myself back on the ground. I could see the faces of those hovering above me. They all looked worried about whether I'd been more successful, but I closed my eyes a moment longer to remember the feelings that consumed me as I was enveloped by the brilliant colors.

After only a moment, I smiled and began to sit up. Cassie handed me a fresh bottle of water and I could see Max eyeing me cautiously, but it was Elizabeth whose face I focused on. One corner of her mouth was curled into a smile and I knew that she realized what I'd seen. She nodded once, then strutted away. I was almost sad to see her go until I heard her call back to us, "call me when you screw this up, I'll see if I can help fix the inevitable mess."

I shook my head while chuckling. Just when you think you're getting somewhere with her, she makes sure to let you know you're not. I looked up at Max and placed my hand on his arm to keep him in place. His anger at her comment was written all over his face. I didn't want him to do something he'd regret. He looked down at me when I touched his arm, and his focus shifted from anger at Elizabeth to concern for me. My heart warmed knowing he was ready to defend me from anyone and that he cared about me enough to ignore his anger at Elizabeth's remarks.

I slid my hand into Max's and let him help me to my feet. I was proud of my accomplishment and wasn't about to let a nasty comment ruin it. I smiled brightly at the group and gave them the play by play of what happened. They all nodded in understanding, so I assumed they went through this process themselves at one point. When I had finished describing my journey, James took over.

"Now that you have a handle on transferring between realms by yourself, we need to build up your endurance. You need to be able to withstand that pressure for longer periods of time before we can add the increased pressure of another person." My stomach was in knots as I anxiously waited for further instructions, this was going to be rougher than all the other training I'd endured over the last several hours. As much as I wanted food for the energy boost, I held out knowing it wouldn't stay in my stomach with a long realm transfer. I settled on an energy drink from the cafeteria that Adam graciously offered to get for me.

The rest of us roamed around another part of the meadow for a few minutes. This area also had several realm doors, and I wondered vaguely why no one was guarding them. It brought back frightening memories of being attacked. I unsuccessfully tried to suppress a shiver at the memory. I closed my eyes to clear my thoughts, but could still see those evil red eyes in the blackness. My eyes flew open and the panic began to rise. I ran my hands up and down my arms to smooth out the goose bumps and took a deep breath.

"You okay?" Max asked, noticing my strange behavior.

"Just nervous I guess," I lied, not wanting to concern him while I scanned my surroundings for any signs of Patroni monitoring the morning activity. "Why aren't these doors guarded? A vampire could sneak right in and no one is here to stop it," I accused, my eyes were growing wider and my voice increasing in decibel to almost yelling.

Cassie grabbed my hand and gave it a small squeeze. "Relax. They're just training doors, no one can sneak in. You're safe here," she explained.

I took a deep breath and rolled my neck, trying to relax. It didn't work. Max placed his hands on the small of my back and used his thumbs to trace small circles repeatedly. Everything melted away like butter on a warm biscuit, and knew it would be okay. I leaned back into him slightly, wanting to feel the heat from his hands but not stop him from tracing the figure eight patterns.

My mind drifted, leaving all thoughts of panic and my training behind, as I began to think of Max. I closed my eyes. This time, the eyes I saw in the darkness were bright blue, warm, and inviting. They crinkled at the sides when he smiled and were framed by thick black lashes. These eyes stared at me in a very different way, wanting only my happiness. They would never cause me fear; instead they would seek a way to right the wrongs I had endured. I felt peacefully calm visualizing them.

What was it about us being near each other that made me feel like my world was complete? Why did I feel such an ache when he was gone for those few weeks? And what secret did he and Cassie hold that they were reluctant to share with me? Before I could think about it any longer, James' voice giving me instructions for my next task pulled me out of my thoughts. I took a few steps forward, reluctantly breaking free of Max's touch. I knew it was the only way to get on with what I needed to do. Adam returned and handed each of us an energy drink as James doled out instructions.

"This is going to be a lot like what you've already experienced, but for a sustained period of time. Remember to keep calm as you go through and you'll be fine. I'm going with you, but I can't touch you or it'll transfer the pressure from you to me. Instead, I'm going to tether your arm to mine so you're within my reach in case something goes wrong. We'll start with five minutes and work our way up to thirty."

"How am I supposed to hold my breath for that long?" It just wasn't possible.

"You're not. You don't need to breathe at all when you're between realms. I know it's a weird concept and one completely foreign to you, but that's why I'm going too. Just focus on me the first time and don't even think about breathing. You're lungs won't be burning for air, so it's just a matter of concentrating."

I thought about this and realized if I had to focus on someone to keep me calm, James was not the best choice for two reasons. First, he was my boss, and I felt a need to impress him. This made relaxing impossible. Second, he couldn't calm me like Max could. How was I supposed to ask for Max instead of James without embarrassing myself or hurting James's feelings? I glanced between the two as I struggled to find the words.

"I think Max should go instead," Cassie blurted out.

My mouth dropped open a little bit realizing what she said. How did she know? She gave me a little wink that only I noticed before addressing James again.

"You should probably get our final timeline from Marco while Max helps her with this part of the training. He's had almost as much experience in changing realms as you. Remember he worked with Marco on that project a few years ago? And besides, we're getting down to the wire and you need to know the final arrangements to coordinate the remaining training schedule. You're better at that stuff than the rest of us."

The last bit of sucking up to his ego was the icing on the cake, and James nodded his head in agreement. I couldn't believe my luck! How had Cassie known I needed Max and not James to help me with this? Sensing this was a good opportunity (and probably the only one I would have for a while) to get information out of her, I decided to take action.

"Hey, can I get a quick bathroom break before we start?" I asked no one in particular, "Cassie, wanna join me?" She skipped towards me and locked arms with me while smiling wryly as we found a ladies room. As soon as the door closed and I knew we had some privacy, I wasted no time in grilling her for information. "Care to tell me what that was all about?"

"I don't know what you mean," she replied aloofly.

"Cass, we don't have time for this. How did you know I wanted Max there to help me and not James?"

"Because you always want Max there. And because he will help keep you calm in a way James can't. It's what you need for your first few times doing this."

"How do you know that? Why do I feel calmer around him than around anyone else?" My need to understand this connection grew. I knew Cassie had answers, and I was tired of waiting for them.

She sighed, as if weighing whether or not to answer my questions. Finally, she turned towards the sink and began smoothing the eye makeup below her eye where it had smudged slightly. I kept staring at her, not allowing her to back out of this conversation. It was already long overdue. I tapped my foot to show my patience was wearing thin. Instead of answering me directly, she posed another question.

"How do you feel when Max isn't around? When he disappeared for a few weeks?"

I felt a little embarrassed, but if I wanted answers from her I had to be willing to reciprocate. "Empty," I stated, laying my cards on the table.

"The reason I know all of this is because it's written all over your face, Luc. I was with you every day while he was gone and I could see the void it left. The same way I can see how being near him brings you joy."

I thought about what happened when I was with him just a few minutes ago and began smiling again. I wondered if it was obvious to everyone else too.

"You're holding out on me. I know there's something else you aren't telling me. Something more concrete than just the look on my face."

She sighed and turned back around to face me. She grabbed me and hugged me tightly for just a moment before she said, "All in good time" and flitted out the door back towards Adam and Max.

Sarah M. Ross

Thirteen

I left the bathroom irritated she had evaded me once again. When I got back to the group, she was happily canoodling with Adam and purposely avoiding me. I wasn't about to let her off the hook that easily so I said vaguely, "We're not done yet," knowing she'd catch my double meaning. I turned back towards Max and he had already placed one of the tether cords around his wrist and was holding out the other end to attach to mine.

I stretched my hand forward and allowed him to tie it around my wrist. I reveled in his touch. I felt my breath catch when he pulled me closer to him to make it easier to attach the cord. My hand tingled where he touched it and I longed to lace our fingers together. He tied the cord, but his hand didn't move away when he was finished. Instead, it stayed there, his fingers gently grasping my wrist with one hand and his other placed against my palm. I stared at our joined hands, amazed that such a simple thing could bring me so much happiness. The sound of Adam clearing his throat brought us out of our trance and we each let our hands drop to our sides.

"Ready?" Max asked me and I nodded. "Just remember, you don't have to breathe. It's not necessary, though blowing air out does relieve some pressure. Just keep reminding yourself of that while we're in there. Our first session will be five minutes, but we'll do four more, increasing the time with each session until we're in there for thirty minutes. Once you can handle that, we'll try holding hands and I'll let you take some of my pressure."

The thought of Max and I secluded and holding hands made me happy. Even if it was going to be a little painful for me, it would be worth it. We headed to the door and I glanced back at Cassie. She was smiling and I heard her whisper, "You got this," just as I stepped through.

Max quickly let go, and I felt that now familiar intense pressure build. I kept my eyes open, marveling how his dark hair stood out even more against the bright lights. His eyes sparkled and not even the profound beauty of the light could compare to them. I smiled at him, keeping my mouth shut to reserve the oxygen in my lungs. He returned my smile, each of us staring at the other. I longed to reach my hand out and touch him, but I knew in doing so it would defeat the purpose of this whole training experiment.

I continued to stare at Max, realizing this was going to be the key to making it through the challenge. I could stare at him for hours and not even realize time was passing. Unfortunately, my body wouldn't fall in line with my mind. After another minute, I caught myself trying to take a breath. I closed my eyes and chanted the mantra that Max gave me: "I don't need to breathe, I don't need to breathe."

Closing my eyes made it worse, so I snapped them back open and kept looking at Max. If he could do this, so could I. It amazed me how he didn't seem to struggle at all with the extreme pressure and inability to breath. I knew he'd been doing this for a long time, but knowing it and seeing for myself how easy this was for him were different somehow.

The best way to make it through was to focus my energy, so I simply stared at Max the whole time. I lost myself in him. The way his hair curled slightly at the ends and locks hung just below his eyebrow, tickling his top eyelid as he moved his head. The dimple that I adored would deepen and somehow make him more handsome as he smiled. His full, kissable lips that made me yearn just thinking about them. Yeah, I had no problems passing the time this way.

He, too, passed the time by focusing on me. The hardest part of this whole training exercise was resisting the urge to touch him. I caught myself twice leaning towards him or reaching my hand forward, but stopped before he noticed. I was grateful, I didn't want him to think that I was struggling or needed help. I started to wonder how much time we had left when Max tilted his head to the side, letting me know it was time to go back. I nodded once and he clasped my hand, releasing the pressure as I landed with an ungraceful thump back on the grass.

"Well?" Cassie drew out the word as she bounced on the balls of her feet.

"Piece of cake!" I smiled up at her. She helped me to my feet while Adam handed Max and I bottles of water.

"You did amazing in there," Max complimented me and I blushed slightly. "Really. I've never seen anyone take to it with such ease. You're simply amazing Lucy."

The blush deepened on my cheeks at his compliment and I was quick to respond. "I couldn't have done it without you Max. You're the only reason I didn't have a total meltdown in there. You've got to take most of the credit."

"Well, I think you two just make the most perfect team!" Cassie quipped. "Like you're completely and naturally in sync with each other."

I shot her a look that screamed *don't embarrass me* and tried to change the subject.

"So now we try again? Round two?" I asked hastily.

"Yes, we'll move from five minutes to fifteen. I'm skipping ten because you did so well your first time through I think you'll be fine with a bigger challenge." Max grabbed my hand and led me to the doors once more. I handed Adam my now mostly empty sports bottle and took a deep breath to steel my nerves.

"All right, let's do this!" I proclaimed, and I was thrust once again between realms.

That training session ended as easily as it started, and I went right up to the doors to complete the hardest one, thirty minutes. I was confident going in, having breezed through the last two stages. I grabbed for Max's hand, but he didn't take it this time.

"You've been doing so great, Lucy, we want to make sure you can handle anything," he started. "You're going to go with Cassie this time." He took off the tethering rope from his arm. While I was bummed I wouldn't get to spend a half hour enjoying the sight of him, I knew he was right. I needed this and Cassie would look after me just like Max.

"All right, girly, it's just me and you," Cassie greeted me. "Let's rock this!" I laughed and helped her tighten the tether cord. I loved the way she could make me laugh regardless of the situation. I really was lucky to have her as my friend.

We stepped through the doors once more. I was confident this would be no problem, and I would get through it as easily as I got through the other two sessions with Max.

Fourteen minutes in I knew I had a problem. My lungs wanted to take in a breath no matter how many times I told them it wasn't needed. My body began to squirm from the pressure and looking at Cassie did not sooth me like watching Max did. I berated myself internally because if I failed, I would lose the opportunity to do the one thing I wanted most.

Could I really do this? Was I good enough? Could I protect her better than anyone else? Shouldn't I leave this to the experts? Doubts began to weigh me down and panic tried to seep in. I could see the concern on Cassie's face as she gave me a thumbs-up sign, trying to encourage me. I wished she knew sign language like James so I could communicate with her. Instead, I saw her bright smile–as bright as the hues of color all around me–and my doubts began to crawl back into their hole. Mind over matter, that's all this was. I wasn't some weak little girl who let self-doubt ruin my goals. I wouldn't let myself take on a victim status before, and I wouldn't do it now. If I wanted something done, I'd do it. Naysayers be damned!

    I thought about all the people who helped me get this far and I knew it was possible. Anything was possible if I worked at it and didn't give up. Jessica didn't give up when she got her cancer diagnosis, and I was sure she was lying in bed right then refusing to give up even as her body failed her. What I was going through, in comparison, was nothing.

    As my confidence surged, I felt my body react to it. I made it through the final challenge knowing that not only had I rocked the challenge, but I wouldn't fail at the one that counted later that day. I could do it and nothing would stand in my way.

Sarah M. Ross

Fourteen

Cassie and I went back to the Commons to wait on word from James. It was mid-afternoon and fairly empty. We joined Max and Adam for a veg-out session of watching bad reality TV. We snagged two of the oversized leather couches. I knew the final hour was fast approaching. I stuffed my nervousness and grief down. I tried to enjoy this small reprieve with Max, relishing the relaxation while we sat next to each other, his arm around me like it's always belonged there. The three of them thought it was hysterical how ridiculous people were willing to act just to get on TV. They all came from a more prim and proper time period, so watching someone get drunk and fall down at 10:00 AM on the beaches in New Jersey just to get famous had them in stitches. I could only shake my head at how low my generation had taken entertainment.

While they watched, I tried my best to keep from glancing anxiously at the clock. We were only five minutes into the show when James and Marco came through the French doors into the Commons. I jumped out of my seat, anxious and confused. Why was Marco here? Seeing me move, the others stood as well and Max tilted his head slightly in question. I knew he was using Marco's mind reading ability to read thoughts to ask him something, and my suspicion was confirmed when Marco shook his head no.

"Good, you're all here," James greeted us. He looked determined and ready for battle, which increased my anxiety.

"We have some news to share. Marco? You want to take the lead?"

Marco nodded briefly to James and turned to address the rest of us. "We've received some intel that points to the vampires knowing who Lucy is, and they have consequently identified her family."

I sucked in a breath, suddenly filled with dread. "How reliable is it?" I asked shakily.

"That's what we're determining now," Marco replied. "But until we know for sure, we don't think you should go. Cassie and Max will act as Guides for your sister."

"What?!" I shrieked. "You can't do this! I've been training so hard and I'm ready for this."

"It's for the best," James answered with Marco nodding in agreement. I wanted to strangle both of them, but it wouldn't help my cause. I stared at Max for support, but he looked as dumbfounded as I did. I walked around the couch and came toe to toe with Marco. I towered over him and hoped he took that as a sign of my strength.

"Listen, this is what's going to happen," I started, my voice filled with resolve. "Jessica is going to be Guided by the best. Maybe James or Max haven't filled you in, but I can do this. I've trained with Elizabeth and Amelia and both of them said I'm the best new recruit they've seen in centuries. I can create and hold three separate shields while under attack. I will stop at nothing to protect her, and no one will be more determined to keep her safe than me. I'm ready for this and I've earned it. You're not taking it away."

"Yes, I've heard about your abilities. But you said it yourself, 'new recruit'. As in no real experience. Training with people who aren't actually trying to kill you doesn't prove anything. The risk is too great. I can't allow it."

"You said yourself you don't know how reliable this intel is." I countered. "It could simply be a front to scare us. How would any of them know who I am? The only two vampires I've ever been in contact with are dead."

"I'm not sure how they learned your identity; my fear is a spy. I've come to your realm to identify the source, but have not heard any indication in anyone's thoughts yet. This has further complicated the original situation, and I no longer feel it's safe to use you as a Guide. Sending you now is a risk I'm not willing to take. The answer is no," Marco commanded.

He must not have realized who he was dealing with if he thought I would just back down because he said no. I'd find a way around him, go above his head maybe. I'd figure out a way. Max joined me, gently taking my wrist to lead me away from Marco. I turned and focused on his eyes, pleading with him. He pinched his fingers at the bridge of his nose for a moment before speaking.

"Lucy, go back to your Dwelling for a few minutes." he whispered in my ear. "Let me see what I can do." I was hesitant to walk away with things unresolved, but I trusted he could help me. I didn't face Marco or James again before walking away. Cassie hollered for me to wait up and joined me at the staircase.

I didn't speak to her until I had closed the door to our Dwelling and plopped on the couch, throwing a pillow across the room. "That son of a bitch! He can't tell me no because of some stupid rumor. He can't go back on his word!"

Cassie listened as I ranted for several minutes, calling Marco every horrible name I could think of. She sat next to me and asked, "Are you done now? Get it all out?"

I nodded but didn't reply. I needed to vent more, but I knew it would get me nowhere.

"I need a plan," I stated.

"Max, James, and Adam are on your side. If anyone can get through to Marco, they can."

I knew she was trying to make me feel better, but I didn't want to leave my fate in the hands of someone else. "There has to be something I can do. Some way to make him see reason."

"I'm sure he's saying the same thing about you," she laughed, a half smile on her face.

"Well, I'm not the one being unreasonable! I'm not the one going back on my word!" I retorted.

Cassie sighed. I took a minute to gather my thoughts before I continued. "I've got it! I have to go back down and talk to Marco," I told Cassie. She looked perplexed, but didn't try to stop me as I ran back down the stairs.

When I reached the Commons, I could hear the guys arguing before I rounded the corner. While I appreciated their support more than I could ever tell them, this was my problem and it wasn't right to make them fight it for me. They stopped talking when they saw me approach, and Max shook his head.

"I thought I told you to go back to the Dwelling, so I could take care of this?" He sighed.

I winced at his words. It sounded like he was reprimanding a child who wouldn't go to their room. I ignored it and began my plea, hoping I hadn't insulted him by needing to fix things on my own. "Max, I appreciate your help. Really, I do. But I need to do this for myself. Guys give me a minute alone with Marco," I insisted. No one moved, so I took Marco's arm and led him to the other side of the room.

"Marco, we all want the same thing," I began. "Our goal is the same: keep Jessica safe. I know you feel there is a heightened risk by allowing me to go, but I strongly believe your intel is skewed. It's not possible for anyone to know who I am. But, I'm willing to compromise with you in the interest of keeping Jessica safe."

"I'm listening," he snapped.

"What if I can get the best back-up possible? Just to make sure nothing goes wrong."

"Who exactly are you referring to?" he questioned, doubt creeping across his face.

I smiled confidently before revealing my secret weapon. "I can get Amelia Earhart to go with us."

"And what makes you so sure she'd be willing to go along with this?"

"I have my ways," I purposefully did not think of my plan so Marco couldn't read my thoughts. Of course, I'd have to run this by her and pray she went along with it, but I was confident in my plan. "Just let me talk to her. If she agrees, will you let me go?"

"You, Max, and Amelia to Guide one eleven year old child? I don't see why not. But if she doesn't agree, the deal is off. I'm not sending you out there with just Max. He'd be too busy protecting you instead of the child."

"What? That's ridiculous," I scoffed.

Marco didn't answer. He just peered at me with a 'You have no idea' look.

"Give me five minutes. I'll be back with Amelia and she'll tell you herself," I continued, not giving much thought to the look on his face before or giving him time to argue I took off out the doors.

I had no idea where to find Amelia, but the training center and obstacle course seemed like a good places to start. I ran by both, but there was no sign of her. An idea came to me and I could have kicked myself for not thinking of it before. Elizabeth called for Amelia using her bracelet. I just needed to do the same thing, but how to make the connection reach her was beyond me. I was running by a guarded door when I recognized the guard and decided to ask for help.

"Excuse me, Ms. Frank?"

Anne glanced up at me but didn't answer right away. She stared quizzically, probably trying to decide if I was some nosy fan who wanted an autograph or someone with legitimate business. "I was wondering if you could help me out for a minute."

"Go on," she prompted in a thick accent.

"Can you tell me how to use my bracelet to contact another person? I'm still new at this and I need to get in touch with Amelia Earhart as soon as possible."

"And how do I know Amelia wants to see you?" she retorted.

"I've been training with her, and I need her help. I promise she'll want to hear what I have to say," I was not above begging at this point.

She stared at me critically before sighing, "All right, but if she gets pissed, I'm blaming you entirely."

"That's fine," I agreed. She showed me how to use the command screen to pull up a directory of people. After scrolling through, I found Amelia's name and saw that I was connected.

"Amelia?" I spoke into my wrist. "Can you hear me? It's Lucy."

"Lucy?" I heard in my head. It sounded at first like it was coming from my own thoughts, but it wasn't my voice. "Why are you calling me?"

"I need your help. Can you meet me at the main entrance to the Commons right now? It's really important." I could sense her hesitation and she sighed audibly, so I threw in, "James said I could count on you to at least listen." It was the only card I had to play and I hoped it would work. Seeing them flirt made me hopeful she wouldn't want to disappoint him.

"Fine," she grumbled. "Give me a few minutes."

"Please hurry. Time is of the essence."

I thanked Anne, who seemed to have brightened her disposition because she waved goodbye cheerfully as I left. I waved back to her as I hurried towards the Commons. I only had to wait a few seconds after I got there before Amelia came around the corner.

"What's this all about, Lucy?" She questioned.

"First, thank you for coming. I know you said today was your day off, and you probably have other things planned.

But I really need your help," I began. I led her to a small bench just outside the doors and explained the situation. She appeared mildly interested, but I wasn't sure my story alone was enough to convince her. Not only was she giving up a day off, but there was also a potential for danger she probably wanted to avoid. I played my trump card. "Listen, Elizabeth told me you're the best. That's why you're her number two. And the best is what I need right now. I know I'm asking a lot, but I promise I'll make it up to you. And moreover, I promise if you help, not only will I be appreciative, but James will be too. So much so I bet I can get him to thank you personally–with a homemade dinner and a movie."

She turned bright red and stared at her feet. It was obvious she wanted to go on a date with him. I was right! I thanked her repeatedly once she agreed and led her by the arm inside the Commons towards Marco. I wasn't letting go for fear she'd change her mind.

Marco looked somewhat surprised to see her, but covered his emotions quickly. Max simply seemed baffled that Amelia was there, and James grinned sheepishly. "Amelia has agreed to go with us. That makes three of us, Marco, and I expect you to live up to your end of the deal."

"Ahh, clever girl," he commented.

I didn't bother to hide how I recruited her from my thoughts. I just smiled smugly as he tipped his head to me.

"Well played, I'm impressed."

"Thank you," I replied. "But we need to get down to business. What's our final timeline?"

Marco pulled a pocket watch from his jacket and glanced up at me, "You need to leave here in forty-five minutes. You'll arrive about an hour before her spirit is released, and you can Guide her back here. Get in, get out. No family reunions while you're there. That can wait until you return."

"Okay, understood," I nodded. With that, Marco turned and left. After I was sure he was gone, I turned to Amelia and Cassie completely embarrassed by what I was about to ask.

"Um," I whispered quietly. "What does one wear on a mission like this?" I scanned my body, noticing my dirty jeans and the tee shirt I'd sweated in all day not quite feeling it was appropriate.

Amelia just shook her head, but Cassie took my hand and began leading me out. "Come on girl, let's get you changed." She chuckled.

"Of all the things to worry about..." I heard Amelia mutter under her breath. I knew they didn't understand, but this would be the first time I'd seen my sister in months. I wanted to make a good impression– one that told her everything was going to be all right. Plus, it was a way to keep my mind occupied on what was going to happen next. I needed this simple distraction to focus my thoughts on anything but my sister dying.

Back in my room, I tossed items out of my closet into piles at my feet. "Too dressy, too casual, can't fight in it..." I went on. After going through everything and finding nothing, Cassie left the room. When she returned, she had a pair of black skinny jeans that had a stretch to them and a ruffled white blouse with little pink hearts stitched along a bias. It was loose enough that I could easily move but soft and pretty so it didn't look like workout gear.

"Oh my goodness, thank you Cassie! This is perfect!" I hugged her. I quickly changed and added a pair of black ballet flats that had a strap on the ankle to make sure they stayed put.

"You ready for this?" Cassie asked and I nodded. "It's about time. We should go meet Max."

I nodded and gulped audibly. She took my hand and led me downstairs. We met Max and proceeded to one of the big blue Realm doors. I felt better knowing that this one was guarded as Max took my hand.

"I can take some of the pressure on our way down," he offered. "Once we get there, you'll probably see people you know. Remember they can't see you or hear you. I'm going to need you to stay strong. You can't be emotional while you're there. You're doing a job. You can cry all you want when we get back; and I'll get you all the chocolate ice cream you can eat, but not until this is over. You can do this, Lucy, I know you can." He gave my hand a small squeeze to reassure me, but I let his fingers go.

"Thank you Max, but I want to do this on my own. I don't need you to take any of the pressure. I can handle it. I promise to stay strong. I won't let you or Jessica down." He dropped my hand, understanding that I couldn't rely on anyone right now and that I had to find my own strength.

Amelia was right behind us and spoke briefly before we headed through the doors. "I'll be there for back up if you need anything. But I'm letting you take the lead."

"Thanks again Amelia. I can't tell you what this means to me."

We took our positions, and I stepped through the door, feeling the Patronus world slip away as I fell towards earth once more.

Sarah M. Ross

Fifteen

The pressure and beautiful lights were the same, but instead of floating, I felt like I was falling. It must have been because I was actually changing realms rather than practicing. Max was beside me, and I hoped that Amelia was right behind us. The trip lasted around three minutes before we came to a stop at a gray door. I still felt the intense pressure which meant I wasn't completely there yet, but was a little confused on what to do next. I glanced behind me at Max and he stepped towards the door, opening it and stepping aside for me to enter first. Once inside, Max and Amelia quickly followed and the door dropped out of sight. I wondered how we would call it back, but before I could ask I stopped dead in my tracks. A familiar sound filled me with joy. My mom was singing a lullaby.

    I turned to see her lying in the hospital bed next to Jessica, my dad on the other side seated in a chair and holding her hand. Tears brimmed in my eyes, but I quickly blinked them away, remembering what Max told me. Jessica looked so pale I wondered if we made it in time, but the steady but slow beeping of the monitors told me we had.

    Max wrapped his arms around my shoulders from behind, holding me tight. I was comforted by having him there, but wanted nothing more than to leave his safe embrace and go to my family.

"Remember, they can't hear you or see you. We have just a short time before she's ready for us," Max said softly in my ear.

I nodded in acknowledgement, fearing my voice would reveal my weakness right now. Instead, I sank deeper into him and let him hold me.

"She looks just like you," Max continued. "Beautiful just like her sister."

"I'm so worried about my mom and dad," I whispered. "How are they going to get through this?" Looking at them, I could tell that my mom probably hadn't slept in days, and my dad's eyes were red from crying.

"They got through it once. They can do it again. People are a lot stronger than we give them credit for."

"It's just not fair. Why has so much been taken from my family? Losing two children in the same year? What did they do to deserve this?"

"It's not about that, Lucy. This isn't a punishment for your parents."

Before I could respond, the doors to the hospital room opened and my grandparents walked in. They brought coffee for my parents, but Mom refused to even sit up to take it. I moved to my sister's bed and placed my hand over my mom and Jessica's. I know they couldn't feel me, but I hoped it brought them a little comfort. I know it did for me.

"I'm right here, Jess. You're going to be okay. There's nothing to be scared of," I cooed. "Don't cry, Mom. I'll take care of her, I promise. I won't let you down."

I stayed there for a while, taking comfort in being near my family once more. A short time later, I noticed that the monitors were beeping a little more slowly and knew that Jessica was fading. Tears fell openly down Dad's cheeks, and Mom kept singing the lullaby as she lay next to Jessica on the bed. Grandma and Grandpa were holding each other, and I wanted nothing more than to hug them all. A doctor came in quietly and stayed at the back of the room. After a moment he said it was time and to say goodbye.

Mom sat straight up and turned to Jessica, brushing her hand against her soft cheek. "Baby girl, we love you so much, and we're so happy we got to love you for the past eleven years. We were so lucky we got to be your parents. Don't you worry about us, Daddy and I will be fine. You go where you need to be. I know Lucy will be waiting for you and she'll take good care of you. You just be sure to tell her how much we love and miss her too."

Jessica opened her eyes and stared directly at me. I sucked in a breath disbelieving she was actually seeing me. She smiled a small smile and sighed. "Hey Lucy! I've missed you."

Baffled, I turned to Max for answers, but didn't wait for them before I went to her bedside. "I'm right here. It's okay now," I told her. I glanced at Mom and Dad who were searching the room, equally as baffled.

Those were Jessica's last words. She took one last breath, and closed her eyes a final time. A moment later, Jessica was standing next to me taking my hand. I gasped and tears fell down my face at feeling her again. Her hand was warm and soft, and her hair smelled like the baby shampoo she still used. I went to my knees and hugged her tight.

"Hi little one!" I started, calling her by the nickname I gave her as a baby. "I missed you too."

"Hi big one," Jessica replied with a smile, no trace of pain anywhere on her face. "What's going on? Did I die? Or am I dreaming? I can still see Mommy and Daddy and Gram and Gramps."

"Yes, sweetie, I'm afraid you did. But it's okay. I'm going to take you to a place where you'll never hurt again. Everything's going to be all right."

"Will you be there with me?"

I didn't know what to say to that. She wasn't going to become a Patronus, and since she was a child, she didn't even stay on our realm to await a decision. She would simply move to the Alpha, and I wouldn't see her again.

I didn't have to find a reply because Max came over and knelt beside me. "Hi, Jessica. My name is Max. I've heard so many wonderful things about you, and it's very nice to meet you," he said, shaking her hand. "Lucy is here to make sure you go on, but she can't stay with you. She has a very important new job helping all kinds of people. So she has to stay with me for now. You should be very proud of your big sister. I know you're a little scared, but I have it on good authority there will be lots of people who love you where you're going, and they'll take really good care of you until you see your mom and dad again."

I could see the angst on Jessica's face at the idea of not being with me, but she was blushing at Max, and she was too shy to say anything. I guess she took after me in the blushing at Max's gorgeous face department. She turned from Max and tugged on my arm, "But I wanna stay with you, Lucy. I don't want to go anywhere else."

I hugged her tight, relishing in the feel of her again before speaking. "I'm sorry, sweetie. You can't. But we get to be together right now, and you get to know I'm okay, and I'll always be watching out for you. You're going to be fine, I promise. There's nothing to be scared of anymore."

The irony of those words hit me almost as hard as the fist that slammed into my face.

Sixteen

I fell back on the floor and tried to shake away the stars that filled my vision. What had just happened? I scrambled to my feet to assess the situation but was immediately struck again, this time on the side of my face. I rocked backwards but managed to stay standing, glad that my body was stronger as a Patronus. If I'd still been human, my jaw would have been pulverized by that last hit. Instinctively, I swiped my hand around my body, encasing it in a shield in order to have a moment to figure out what was happening. As I took in the room, horror filled me. There were at least a dozen vampires filling the small space. They were strategically placed on every surface available leaving no room for escape. I immediately knew this was a planned attack.

Crap! I thought to myself. *I should have taken Marco's warnings more seriously. How am I going to get us out of this?*

The vampires formed semi-circles around Max and Amelia, essentially backing them into a corner so they couldn't get away from the blitz attack. Max had been hit in the ambush as well and was on his hands and knees struggling to stand back up. I could see a small trickle of blood oozing from his lip and feared for what would happen to him. Amelia had shoved Jessica far behind her in the corner and was now fighting three of the creatures at once. It was weird to see the vampires moving around the room, weaving in, through, and between my family members who stood by unaware of the battle raging all around but parallel to them. I moved in front of Jessica and dropped the shield that surrounded me. I transferred it to Jessica and created a second for Max. Powering two shields now made it hard to fight offensively, but it was my only choice.

Several of the vampires came at me, snarling viciously with their fangs elongated in anticipation. Jessica cried softly, but I couldn't worry about that. I conjured a silver dagger in one hand and a silver glove for the hand that held the shields, so they couldn't touch it to make me drop them. I further readied myself with silver toed boots and a silver studded choker so they wouldn't be tempted to bite me. I wished I could have made a silver body suit, but it would be too heavy for battle.

Max had gotten back up by that time and indicated he was ready to attack, and I could drop his shield. I did so and watched him thrust and jab at anything that came near him. Amelia was weakening from fighting so many, so I placed a shield around her to give her a reprieve while she regained her strength.

The battle raged on for what seemed like hours. Every time Max or Amelia would knock one down, three more would take its place. Both of them were bleeding heavily from scratches and bite marks, but neither gave up the fight. I alternated putting shields on one or both of them, but when I did the vampires they were fighting would just come after me instead. I had no less than two vampires on me at every turn. My silver gear helped to protect me, but they still found ways to gouge at my back or bite my thighs. I kicked and flung Chinese throwing stars, but it never seemed to be enough. Sweat dripped off me and I wobbled on my feet, exhausted from shielding for so long. I didn't know how much longer I could continue and prayed that I had the strength to protect Jessica just a little while longer.

After a while, they seemed to deduce that Jessica was directly behind me. Even though they couldn't see her, they attempted to pierce my shield with everything they had—fangs, claws, weapons—in order to get to her.

"Jess, I need you to go to the place where I always found you during hide and seek. Go there and don't move until I come for you," I screamed at her, praying she remembered that as a toddler when we played the game, she'd always hide in the shower. My shield could keep her hidden even in another room and hoped it was enough to keep the trail off of her for a while longer.

As scared as she was, she ran right towards the small hospital bathroom. I didn't look at her for fear that one of the vampires would notice which direction she headed and try to seek her out. Without Jessica in the corner to protect, I advanced into the fray. I dropped all shields except for the one around Jessica. Max, Amelia and I formed a triangle, protecting each other's back as we rotated around the room. Amelia seemed more determined than ever to kick some serious vampire butt. The intense look on her face made me glad she was on my side. She conjured up two guns, Colt 45s, and loaded them with silver bullets. I followed suit with a Walther PPK like I'd seen Elizabeth use. It was smooth and well-balanced in my hand. I'd only practiced shooting a gun a few times during my weapons training, and each time I barely hit the target. I was apprehensive about my abilities, but there was never a better time to start trying than now.

Max opted for a bow and silver arrows, which I thought was a weird choice for such an enclosed space, but I trusted he knew what he was doing. Amelia gave a silent signal and we fired simultaneously. Bullets flew and arrows pierced the vampire's flesh. I quickly fired again, knowing I was having the most trouble hitting a target. The noise caused a ringing in my ears, and I struggled to keep my hands from shaking. Four vampires had fallen and were in a pile at our feet. I knew they were only stunned and not dead, but I still took a grotesque pleasure at kicking them. I saw Max load arrow after arrow, and Amelia fired like a trained marksman hitting target after target, but it only seemed to slow them down. Why weren't they falling? Two more fell, but six more entered the room. Apparently their back up had arrived. We were in serious trouble.

Max yelled for me to put shields back up. I dropped my gun, which melted away, and threw up shields around the three of us. I whipped my head around the room, taking in the situation. My breath started to hitch. My eyes, now wide with fear, begged Max and Amelia for answers, but they looked just as lost as I did.

"Now what?" I asked, my voice cracking and raising half an octave to betray my panic and glad the shields were also soundproof to the vampires.

"We need to formulate a plan, and quickly," Max replied, "The longer we stay invisible, the more time they have to gather reinforcements and possibly discover wherever Jessica is hiding. Is your shield around her still solid?"

"Yes, I even reinforced it," I responded, "but I'm exhausted and don't know how much longer I can keep it up. Adrenaline can only take me so far. I'm afraid I'm going to pass out like I did in practice. Amelia, please tell me you have a plan. Can we get that door thing to come back while we're still shielded and just slip away before they realize we're gone?" It was the best idea I could come up with.

"Unfortunately no, Lucy," she responded sadly before explaining, "the door is designed not to appear if a vampire is sensed in the area. And with this many, there's no chance it'll show up. We would have to get rid of them all first. And we can't call for back up because our bracelets don't allow us to communicate while on Earth, only on our realm. Our only option is to fight."

I hung my shoulders, and Max sighed deeply. It really was the worst case scenario. My meager training had not prepared me for this.

"Here's what we're going to do. Lucy, keep the shield around you. Max and I will split up around the room while we're still shielded to get the element of surprise. Max, drop the bow. You need something stronger now. I say high powered rifle. I'll double up on my Colts, and I recommend silver hollow points to inflict maximum damage."

Max nodded and took his position at the doorway leading to the main hospital. Amelia moved to the opposite end near the bathroom where Jessica was hiding. They nodded to each other that they were ready.

I was about to drop the shields when Amelia gave one final instruction, "Aim for the heart. It'll keep them down the longest. When enough of them are down, Max and I can take them on our own. Lucy, I want you to conjure syringes and suck as many souls into them as you can. Listen for my go signal."

I heard Max cocking his rifle and knew we were ready to go. I made sure I had my gun ready and nodded. "On three," she announced. "One… two… THREE!" I dropped the shields and pulled the trigger. I fired over and over again, praying I'd hit a target. I aimed for the largest target, their chests, but repeatedly hit nothing or merely grazed an arm. This was a small room, so I thought I'd hit something, but with moving targets it was so much harder. I really wished I'd trained with guns rather than knives earlier in the week. Holding that thought, I dropped the gun and conjured bowie knives instead. I knew I was more accurate with them. I threw as fast as I could conjure them. Vampires were falling left and right, but there were still too many. Not enough were falling for me to start my work with the syringes.

I turned in circles, essentially dancing with my targets as I impaled them with the knives. I knew we were gaining momentum and almost smiled at the thought. Vampire bodies were scattered around the room and some were even being used as shields to keep their comrades unharmed. Amelia and Max were brilliant, leaving a path of destruction in their wake and I finally heard Amelia call, "Now, Lucy! We've got you covered."

I threw my last two knives at the vampire in front of me and watched the evil grin on his face fade as the point of the knife connected. He fell to the floor moaning. He was the first soul I would retrieve. I plunged the long thin needle directly into him and pulled up on the plunger, proud that I was saving the soul of someone who hadn't chosen or deserved to live like this.

I finished, placing the now capped syringe in my satchel and moved on to the next closest vampire to me who seemed to be incapacitated. He had multiple bullet wounds and probably would not be moving for quite a while, therefore posing no imminent threat. I quickly retrieved the soul and moved on to get a third. While on my knees moving around the room, a vampire tried to bite me from above. I smelled the rancid breath coming from his rotting teeth as he dropped towards me. I plunged the syringe into the vampire below me with one hand while simultaneously piercing my knife into the neck of the vampire coming from above with the other.

We were doing it! We were going to make it! I was almost giddy and I slid on the now blood covered floor to the next fallen vampire to retrieve his soul. Just as I plunged the tip of the needle into his chest, I heard Jessica scream. I wheeled away from the vampire and scrambled to my feet. Had my shields failed? Yes, I was exhausted and on the brink of collapse, but adrenaline was keeping me strong. I made it to the bathroom entrance when I felt a searing pain in the back of my head, and the world went black.

Seventeen

My eyes fluttered. I could sense a brightness in front of them and knew that I was laying on my back, propped against something soft. Something wet was dabbing my head and a cold drop trickled down my neck, causing goose bumps to form. I forced my eyes open, squinting as they painfully adjusted to the light.

"Max? Jessica?" I called. I was on the ground back in my realm just in front of the door we'd originally transferred to earth in. A balled up sweatshirt was under my head forming a make-shift pillow, and Amelia was dabbing a washcloth on my head. A little farther away, Max paced restlessly.

"Max? Where's Jessica?" I called again. He ignored me, balling his fists as he continued wearing down a path in the grass as he paced, kicking small stones and tree stumps as he went.

"Someone tell me what's going on," I begged, my heart racing. My eyes darted between the two, finally settling on Amelia, suspecting since she was closest (and not seething with anger) that she might give me some answers.

"You were struck from behind and rendered unconscious. Your shield on Jessica dropped. We weren't able to get to her in time. The vampires surrounded us, and we couldn't break through," Amelia explained, a single tear now falling from her eye. "We did everything we could. Everything. But as soon as you were knocked out, they swept her up and she was gone. She's gone, Lucy. I'm so sorry."

While I heard her words, I refused to believe them. I staggered to my feet, screaming her name as I searched the field. She had to be here. Maybe she was still hiding and afraid to let Amelia know she was here. I screamed until my voice was raw. I screamed until I fell to my knees, weak from the battle I endured. I screamed until it came out as nothing more than a whisper. Then I silently screamed until I had no more strength. Max knelt next to me and wrapped his arms around me.

"It's my fault," he cried. "I'm so sorry. She's gone, Lucy. But we'll find her, I promise."

The pain in my chest exploded as my heart broke into a million shards. My eyes rolled back in my head, and I collapsed. The world mercifully faded away.

Eighteen

I was awake again, but I was in a world I no longer wanted to be a part of. The emotions that raged through me were crushing my soul so fiercely that I sobbed uncontrollably once again. I didn't know how to handle them and crying was the only outlet I could take. Max looked horrified as buckets of tears flowed from my eyes and I hyperventilated. He frantically searched for someone to help–having no idea what to do with a hysterical woman losing her mind in public. I wasn't in enough control to explain what I needed and I didn't have the answer anyway. I couldn't form any coherent words, so I just focused on him. I stared at the radiant blue of his eyes while he scanned the area. The beauty of them made me tremble and I sobbed harder. Max scooped me in his arms and held me close as he ran back towards the Dwellings. Maybe he was taking me to Cassie or James for help or just to my own room so I could break down privately. It didn't matter; I couldn't care about inconsequential things while wrapped in his arms. I clung to him as a drowning person would a life vest. I had no idea why my body reacted so strongly now, but I knew that the solution was having him near me. He ran swiftly, murmuring soothing sounds in my ear. He was trying to calm me down, but the sweet softness of his voice only made my body want to scream. I must have been having a nervous breakdown. Surely they would lock me in a padded room or some Patronus equivalent. I knew nothing I was doing made any type of logical sense, but logic was no longer controlling my body.

We made it to the Commons, and Max paused inside briefly as he scanned the room. He must not have found what he was looking for because we took off again towards my Dwelling. I saw the expressions on the faces of a few people as we passed by and wondered briefly what I must look like to them. Glancing down at myself, my shirt was soaking wet with tears, sweat, and blood. The shirt clung to me, causing goose bumps to form on my arms. As we passed by a mirror, I saw my reflection for the briefest of moments. Black mascara was running down my face and my hair was a tangled mess. I looked like a Halloween prop in a haunted house. And of course, this made me cry even harder.

Max stopped running and leaned me down to use the arm supporting my legs to open the door to my Dwelling. He paused again briefly inside, I assumed to find Cassie. Seeing no one, he went straight to my room and gently laid me on the bed. With his arms no longer around me, I felt cold and began to shiver. He took both of his hands and held my face in them, searching for answers in my eyes.

"Please Lucy, tell me what I can do," he pleaded. "I don't know how to help you. I know you feel as though this is your fault, but it's not. You can't blame yourself. We'll get her back. I promise you. I'll do anything to make it better. Please just tell me what to do. I can't stand to see you in this much pain!"

I couldn't answer. I couldn't even begin to form words. I was too lost in my emotions. They overpowered every part of me and were in complete control. I needed to go to a place without thoughts of Jessica, helpless and trapped by vampires with her soul ripe for thievery. I needed to feel something other than grief for a few minutes. The solution suddenly came to me. I needed to kiss Max. I had to escape into him and have the only feeling that ran through me be one created by his sensual touch. I couldn't wait any longer. The need to feel him touch me and taste me engulfed my senses. I pressed my body up against his, reveling in the jolts of electricity that flowed through me as we touched. I didn't want to wait for a slow build up or a gentle exploration of my lips. I needed the heat of his skin against mine, the stubble on his cheek to scratch me as his mouth tasted its way down my body.

But this was Max. No matter how much I needed him, I knew he wouldn't do anything out of fear he was taking advantage of me when I was vulnerable. I just had to touch him, feel connected to him in a way that made everything else seem trivial. I wanted to lean into him, trusting him to take over and just let go of everything else.

I gazed into his eyes, searching them. I raised my fingertips until they came to rest on his face, gently gliding one finger over the softness of his lips. Our eyes stayed locked, and I could see the yearning and passion in his. I knew he wanted this as much as I did. I traced over the hills and valleys of his chest and abs and felt his thick callused hands sliding down my bare arms, leaving a tingle in their wake. The heat rose between us until it became almost overpowering. He leaned into me, almost lying on top of me. I felt solace having his strong body so close to mine. He stopped abruptly but didn't move.

"Oh, Lucy, I can't do this now. It wouldn't be right. I care about you too much."

I didn't reply. Instead I pulled him even closer to me. He came willingly, holding me tight now and resting his forehead against mine. His warm breath tickled my cheek. I crushed my lips to his, rejoicing in the union. He eagerly returned my kiss, and I let go of all thoughts except for of this wonderful moment with Max. His hands cupped my face and tilted my head back, giving him more access. The scent of his sweat mixed with a touch of musky cologne engulfed my nostrils and my heart pounded even harder in my chest.

My eyes slid closed, I was only with Max now and wouldn't let any outside thoughts try to creep in. I'd been drawn to Max like a magnet since first arriving, and now that we were together I never wanted to be apart. I moaned with delight as his tongue greedily explored my mouth. He tasted of sweet plums with a hint of mint. His soft lips trailed down my neck, causing the most intense longing I'd ever felt. I loved kissing Max. My body was warm all over and we sizzled with electricity where our bodies touched.

As he kissed me, I began to see flashes of images in my mind. Bright red, then a flash of skin from someone I didn't recognize. Lush green trees and vines and then an image of a dry, barren desert. I shook my head to clear the thoughts and concentrated on the feel of Max's lips as we kissed, but the images only grew more prominent. They felt like memories, but I didn't recognize anything in them. They came in rapid succession and overwhelmed me.

He must have noticed my hesitation because he stopped and leaned up, peering deeply into my eyes. "Lucy, what is it? Are you okay?"

"I'm fine; I feel wonderful now," I reassured him, running my fingers through his thick hair. I pulled him back towards me inch by inch and marveled at the electricity that sparked once again as our lips touched.

After a few more moments of kissing, he smiled at me, gently brushing my fingers against his own calloused ones. "I'm here for you, and I want you to know I'm not going anywhere ever again. We'll get her back, my darling, I swear this to you."

At his well intended words, I forgot about the strange images and the tears started again. Max let go of my face and wrapped me back up against his body, rocking me while his fingers gently combed through my hair. I could feel his lips on my forehead as he continued to murmur soothing noises.

We stayed that way until my tears slowed. I could see the light from the window changed and was growing darker. Hours must have passed. I began hiccupping loudly. I tried to steady my breathing, but still I could not speak. His fingers twined in my hair and his lips remained on my forehead. His tight hold of me never wavered though he must have been tired.

    I heard Cassie come home, but Max never called for her. He must have been too concerned about starting me crying again with a new distraction. He was probably right. My eyes eventually began to feel heavy, and I struggled to keep them open. I didn't want to fall asleep and wake up without Max. I fought to keep that from happening, but I eventually lost the battle, falling into a troubled sleep.

Sarah M. Ross

Nineteen

It had to have been a dream—no a nightmare. My sister was safe. I had rescued her. She hadn't been captured by vampires so they could turn her into a bloodsucking monster. I kept my eyes closed, hoping to delude myself for just a little while longer. I could feel reality setting in as the memories rushed back to into my mind. I tried to push them back down, not ready to face what had happened. My head was still resting on Max's chest. I tried to focus the even sounds of his breath as he slept. In the back of my mind, I knew yesterday actually happened and dealing with it today might be even worse. My emotions were more under control, but I began to feel panicky realizing my own selfishness caused all of this. And there would be consequences.

While I lay comfortably next to Max, confusion replaced the panic as the strange images began to pop up again. As I'd drifted off to sleep the night before, they plagued my dreams. The images were of people I'd never seen, yet they seemed familiar. They ran naked and frolicked in a place I'd never been. Trees covered with moss and vines, gardens and fields that were teeming with wildlife. I'd never experienced such a strange sense of familiarity and confusion at the same time.

I was still consoled by Max being there. I felt warm encased in his arms and could have stayed there forever, but that desire paled in comparison to my need to kill anything that stood in the path of my rescue of Jessica. I needed time alone to think and clear my head of guilt so I could formulate a plan. I needed to do this alone, and I knew Max wouldn't just let me go. He'd want to talk to me about what happened and give me more bull about how it wasn't my fault. Of course it was! I was the only one to blame for this fiasco.

How was I going to be able to leave without waking him up? I ever so slowly turned my face to behold him—just to make sure he was still sleeping, I lied to myself. He looked peaceful. The corner of his mouth turned up in a crooked smile, and I momentarily forgot why I wanted to run away. I tried to gently duck my head from under his arm, but my long hair got caught in Max's hand that had been caressing me last night. Damn it! I knew I should have gone for the pixie cut! I took a sharp breath and tugged on my hair, ignoring the pain at the roots as it pulled. The pain in my head was the least of my worries.

It worked! I collected my hair in a knotted bun and secured it with a tie I always kept on my wrist just in case. I crept towards the door and carefully turned the knob, inching the bedroom door open just enough to squirm my body through. I looked back at Max sleeping in my bed and felt like screaming. It was the perfect sight and what I'd been dreaming about for weeks, Now I was running away from him.

Once in the living room, I quietly put on my shoes and grabbed a pullover to cover my still damp tee shirt. Looking down, I noticed it was not only covered with blood, but also stained with mascara. I tiptoed out the front door and closed it behind me. Now what? It's not like I could hide forever from the nightmare I created. I leaned against the doorframe weighing my options on what to do next. Just as I was about to head to the training center, the door opened behind me and I fell back through it, straight onto my butt. Cassie stood over me smiling.

"You've *got* to stop sneaking up on me, Cassie!" I barked as quietly as I could to make sure I didn't wake up our neighbors or more importantly, Max.

Cassie didn't reply. She helped me up and pulled me into the hallway, closing the door quietly behind us. She grabbed my hand and led me towards the Commons.

"What are you doing Cass? Where are you taking me?" I asked, panic evident in my voice. I wasn't ready to face people yet.

"I want to talk to you," was the only answer she gave me. We kept walking until we reached the library room in the commons. Thankfully, it was vacant at this hour. Cassie shut the door behind us to make sure we weren't interrupted and we each took an oversized armchair.

"Okay, first," Cassie started before wrapping me in a big hug, one which she didn't let me escape. "Oh sweetie! I'm so sorry about everything." She cooed like I was a small child. "How are you feeling? Are you okay? I've been so worried about you."

I smiled at her, thankful for her unnecessary concern and puzzled by how she knew already. "How did *you* hear? Max didn't leave me to get you and we hadn't told anyone or been debriefed."

"Um…well…word kinda got around," Cassie admitted. "It's not often that someone is carried through our realm, bawling hysterically. So people started asking questions. Someone probably asked Marco, and he told them. Well, that and Amelia told James when she saw him last night. I tried to come in to see you, but when I opened your door you were asleep on Max, and he whispered that you were okay, but not to wake you." She explained.

I was mortified. It was even worse than I'd imagined. Now everyone knew what a royal screw up I was. I was most likely going to get fired for my disastrous failure. "Oh. My. God." I choked out. Cassie quickly continued in effort to placate me.

"It's not as bad as I'm making it sound. I'm sorry. I'm going about this all wrong. No one thinks you're to blame. Everyone understands you did your best. We can't win every time. We're all just worried about you. Would you like to talk about what happened yesterday?"

Taking a deep breath, I started, "I have no idea where things started to go wrong. We were fine one minute—I was hugging Jessica and explaining to her what was happening. The next minute there were vampires everywhere trying to kill us and steal Jessica. I put up as many Shields as I could, but there were just too many of them."

I continued to give her the details of our brutal attack and how I'd failed miserably when I was needed most. She listened without interrupting to placate me, for which I was grateful. I couldn't stand to hear another person tell me it wasn't my fault or I wasn't the one to blame. Instead, she just held my hand and squeezed it tight whenever my voice would crack.

"Cassie, we had to have been set up. They had to know I was coming. But how? Marco said he was going get word out that I wasn't going and that it wasn't even my sister. Only those in this realm knew the truth. Cass, I hate to say it, but I think someone here ratted us out to the vampires."

"No! Lucy, another Patronus would never do that."

"Then explain to me how they knew when to ambush us?"

"I…I can't. But I'll help you get to the bottom of this, you have my word."

"I knew I could count on you, Cassie."

Cassie didn't say anything for a minute, but instead gave me another strong hug. After a few minutes, she asked quietly, "Can you finish the story?"

I nodded and took a deep breath, remembering where I left off. "When I came to, Amelia told me they'd knocked me out and my shield had failed. It was too late, Jessica was gone. That's when I lost it and started crying hysterically. I kept telling myself 'Get a grip, you don't have time to break down now. Stop crying already!', but I couldn't make myself stop. It's like I'd been bottling up all of my emotions since I got here, and losing Jessica was the Mentos that caused my Coke to explode."

My analogy obviously went over her head based on the confused expression on her face (age gap! I kept forgetting!).

"Oh Lucy! Why didn't you come to me before now if you were feeling upset? That's what I'm here for silly!"

"I guess I didn't even realize I'd been bottling things up, including my feelings for Max. I still can't figure out why I feel so strongly for him. I have ever since I got here, and it makes no sense. We're not dating; we've only spent a little time together—so why did I feel like my world was exploding when he asked to be reassigned? Why did that bother me so much when he was gone for those two weeks?" I pleaded. I needed some answers to make sense of the chaos that surrounded me. "Then, last night we finally kissed, and it was amazing. Mind blowing, earth shattering kissing. I swear there was actual electricity between us that caused sparks to fly. Literal sparks! My lips still burn a little. Then, even weirder, I kept getting flashes of strange pictures in my head while we kissed and all night while I slept. They were filled with strange places I've never been and people I've never met, but they felt so familiar." I paused a moment before begging, "Cassie, please don't hold back on me now. I can't keep feeling this way and not having a single idea why. It's driving me insane and I can't handle these emotions on top of my emotions about yesterday. It's just too much."

Cassie looked pensive as she played with strands of her hair. I could tell that she was uncomfortable answering me but if she really wanted to help me, answers were what I needed. I gave her a few more seconds before audibly groaning.

"Okay, okay," she said and sat more upright in her seat. "I'll tell you what I know, but I really don't think I'm the person you should be asking. You really should talk to Max."

As if her words granted the wish, Max stepped through the door.

"There you are! I was so worried when I realized you left, Luc. Why didn't you wake me?" Max fretted.

"I needed some time by myself to think. I'm really sorry about yesterday. I don't know where it went wrong, but I realize it's my fault." I squirmed in my seat and fidgeted with my hair. This confrontation was due, but I was hoping to be well buried under my rock of shame before it actually happened.

"Luc," Max started. "Please talk to me. I want to help." I didn't answer—because honestly what could I say. With the mess I'd created, I was beyond help. What I did know was that I involved Max in this mess and I owed him an apology.

"Before you say anything Max, I need to say how sorry I am for yesterday and to thank you for being there for me. I should have never put you in that position. You were kind to help me with my selfish need to see Jessica one last time." I sighed and blinked away tears. He kissed my forehead and let me continue. "It wasn't fair for me to expect you would do this for me, and I shouldn't have asked. I'm too new and I should have left the mission to the experts. At least then Jessica would be safe now. It was my fault we were attacked yesterday and then I went and unloaded everything on you when we returned. I bottled up my feelings recently, and they flooded out after we got back yesterday. I'm sorry."

"It's okay, Luc, part of this is my fault," Max admitted. "We've needed to talk about some things now for a while. I hoped for a better time to have this conversation, but I don't see this getting any easier, so I'm just going to tell you." He sighed.

"I'll leave you two alone for a bit." Cassie said as she tiptoed out the door, closing it behind her.

Max closed the shades so no one could see in and we were all alone again. He sat next to me and took my hands in his. He took a breath and actually squirmed in his seat. I'd never seen him look this nervous, and I squinted my eyes trying to fathom what the cause might be.

"Lucy, how do you believe the universe came into existence?" he began. It was an odd question and I bit my lip trying to keep from laughing at it.

"Huh? What does that have to do with the price of tea in China?"

"Now we're talking about tea?" he asked, clearly confused.

"Never mind," I responded, moving on. "What do my beliefs about the creation of the universe have to do with my strong connection to you?"

"Everything," he stated simply. I waited for him to continue, but he didn't so I answered to appease him.

"Well, I believe that God made the universe. But not like it is today. I think God started it, but things have still evolved naturally over the billions of years. Does that answer your question?"

"And what of the first people who roamed the planet? Do you believe we started out as monkeys?" he pressed. I shook my head at this strange line of questioning but answered, hoping that once we got passed this he'd get back to me and him.

"No. I don't. I think some things have evolved, but humans did not evolve from an amoeba or whatever. I think people have always been people. Maybe more primitive people, but still people. I'm really confused Max," I admitted.

"You're right Lucy. God did create people unique and separate from animals. In fact, the deep, overwhelming love that couples feel for each other evolved as well. From the original couple."

"You mean Adam and Eve?"

"That is what they were called in the biblical story, but it was even much deeper of a connection than historians wrote. They were literally two halves of the first soul that God created. Soul mates. They completed one another and loved so intensely it can no longer be imagined, because no other two people have ever been that connected. They are the only couple in all of creation who have ever been equal halves of one whole. If you take all of the love stories ever written, from Catherine and Heathcliff, Romeo and Juliet, Elizabeth and Mr. Darcy and even Scarlett and Rhett—their love is only a fraction of what the original couple felt.

All of their descendents carry with them a piece of that love from the original souls, and it's gradually gotten smaller as the centuries passed. When two people who have a small piece of that come together today, they feel as if they are soul mates. Because they are, just at a smaller level. No one could ever duplicate what the original two had.

"So you're saying that we have a piece of that?" I pressed. "It feels so much more intense than just what a tiny piece could account for. I know you feel it too."

"You're right, Lucy. I do feel it just as strongly as you do. And it has killed me every day not to convey that to you. But I had to explain this to you first before I could act on my feelings. But there's more. When the original couple betrayed God, they lost their immortality and died. But a soul, as we both know, doesn't die. So God allowed their souls to live on earth again, each seeking its mate for a chance to be reunited. This opportunity has been made possible numerous times, but rarely have the souls been reunited with each other. Lucy, the souls have finally been reunited in us. We are those soul mates. And we're together again, finally."

Max sat silently as I tried to take this all in. I had so many questions, my mind reeled. What did this mean?

Max and I weren't just soul mates; we were the original soul mates that started it all. Our destiny was to seek each other out through the millennia in order to be complete. It explained so much of how I felt but left me with a million questions. I was glad he was holding me as what he told me began to sink in. How was all of this possible?

And to that end, was this—all of this—my fault? Did he blame me for literally ruining the world? Had I been the source of all the pain in the world because I wanted to eat an apple? Is that why I hated eating them to this day? Was Jessica dying and getting captured my fault for bringing sin into the world? Did God hate me for my poor choice eons ago and was now doling out my punishment? Was this Karma coming back and biting me? Lifetime after lifetime?

I turned to Max, picking one of the now innumerable questions that now raced in my head to start with. For unknown reasons, it seemed like the most important.

"Do you love me?"

"I never stopped," he replied simply. "I love you now more than ever."

"I…"

Before I could reply, Marco burst into the room and skidded to a stop a la Risky Business, just not only in his underwear. "She's been spotted!" he interjected.

Max grabbed my hand and we ran for the realm doors.

Sarah M. Ross

To be continued in book two:

Avenge

Coming Late Summer/Fall 2012

About the Author

Sarah M. Ross started her obsession with reading at an early age, getting in trouble for sneaking Baby-Sitters Club and Nancy Drew books into math class in elementary school. She would read any fiction book she could get her hands on. She knew it was an addiction when instead of grounding her from TV or music, her mom would take away her books as punishment (The Horror!).

Her love of all things paranormal was inspired by her good friend Laurie, who convinced her that books with vampires, witches, and all things shifter were amazing. After a little reluctance, she gave it a shot with the Sookie

Stackhouse books, realized her friend was right, and the rest was history.

Ms. Ross grew up in Pittsburgh, graduated from the University of Pittsburgh with a degree in English, and taught 8th graders to love reading as much as she does for several years.

She will always be a proud member of Steelers Nation, but couldn't take the cold and moved her frozen tush to Florida where she now lives with her family and two cats.

You will find her many days with her trusty Kindle in hand and toes in the sand!

Acknowledgment

This book would not have been possible without the love and support of so many people. Words alone cannot express my gratitude, but I thank you nonetheless.

First, thank you to everyone in HP's Writing Group and the IC. Without your continued advice and support, this would still be a pipe dream.

To my critique partners, Wenona and Melanie, you have helped keep me sane when I felt like going crazy. And without you, this book would most likely not be what it is today.

Extra special thanks go to Margaux, who kept me going when I needed it most. You are brilliant and truly a wonderful friend. Theodore Roethke and Ulin would be proud.

Thank you to my Beta readers, especially Sheraya. You let me know that Awaken had an audience and for that I am grateful.

To the wonderful ladies at 4 Corners Press, who helped make my dreams come true. Thank you for taking a chance on me.

Thanks to my editor, Matthew Rush, who put up with my insanity.

To my sister, Jessica, who let me kill her. I always wanted to be an only child! Love you!

And finally, to Steve and my family. Thanks for not giving up on me and for believing in my dream.